THE PRIZE

A CONTEMPORARY REVERSE HAREM ROMANCE
(SAVAGE MOUNTAIN MEN)

MIKA LANE

ISBN ebook 978-1-948369-32-9
ISBN print 978-1-948369-33-6

Like deals and other cool stuff?
Sign up for my newsletter!

CHAPTER 1

ALESSIA

"*I* can't *breathe*."

Giggles fluttered through the crowd. Eight grown-ass women gathered around me drowning in yards of baby pink tulle and other frills comprising the hideous gowns of my bridesmaids.

You'd think I'd be used to the dresses by now. Not in *love* with them, but at least *resigned* to them.

Personally, I wouldn't have been caught dead in something that looked like a five-year-old's idea of a princess party outfit.

But, my vote didn't count.

Even though it was *my* wedding.

One of the bridesmaids behind me—I wasn't sure

which since I scarcely knew most of them—was pulling on the strings of my lacy white bustier—the top of my wedding dress. Her torture was stealing my last breath and probably rearranging my internal organs.

I was in the best shape of my life, but that didn't stop the 'wedding pros' from trying to make my waist smaller, and my boobs bigger.

Another thing I had no say in.

The stylist, hired just for the occasion, sighed loudly and impatiently, looking me up and down while throwing out instructions to everyone in the room. "It's not working. The boobs have to be pushed up more."

I gestured to my shrinking waistline. "I look fine. Can't we call it done?"

Eight pairs of eyes hooded in mink eyelashes and heavy makeup looked at me in horror. If I weren't the bride, they might have ganged up and beaten me.

Well, except for my best friend, Lady. She looked around nervously, torn between wanting to support me and preserving her own well-being amongst the wedding zealots.

The stylist waved her hand. "Untie it. Untie it now."

Whew. Thank god.

Not so fast.

"Okay. This is what we're gonna do." She reached into what she called her 'magic bag' and pulled out a roll of caution tape.

Yup, caution tape. Like the kind used to cordon off hazards like sinkholes or condemned houses.

Kind of like the situation I was facing at that very moment.

She ripped off a piece about twelve inches long. What the fuck? Was she going to put it over my mouth and nose to suffocate me because I couldn't be satisfactorily squeezed into her idea of what a 'perfect bride' looked like?

"Pull it down," she said simply, gesturing at the bustier with her chin.

More titters.

"Huh?"

She rolled her eyes and gestured with her head. "Pull the top down. I need to get at your bosom."

What? Why?

But I obeyed, and she came at me with that damn yellow and black tape, putting one end of the piece on the outside of my right boob, carrying it under both boobs, and securing it on the other side of my left boob. The girls were now essentially taped together, creating a shelf of cleavage I didn't know they were capable of.

Seriously. They were not only squished together but also about three inches higher than where they normally lived on my chest.

Which I guess was the desired look.

"Okay. Now we can redo the bustier." She pulled it up and over my new boob shelf.

With every movement, the tape tugged on my delicate skin.

"I don't know about this. It's not comfortable—" I said politely.

"*Hush,*" she said, as someone behind me started pulling on the laces again.

And while I ended up back where I had been minutes earlier—but even *more* uncomfortable—I was, again, left wondering why I had to be tied into something that restricted my breath. But everyone else in the room nodded and sighed with great satisfaction as the bustier took on the shape it had been created for.

Too bad it wasn't the shape of my body. Or the natural shape of it, anyway.

But like I said, *my* vote didn't count.

My ability to breathe didn't, either.

"Okay, everybody," my best friend and maid of honor, Lady, said to the crowd, none of whom she'd ever met until just a couple days ago, "let's toast our beautiful Alessia, star winner of *The Mating Game* and soon-to-be wife of the handsome, successful, and rich Montgomery Langton—"

"Wait," a tall, thin blonde interrupted.

Vanessa.

She'd been on the show with me, and while Mont the bachelor had chosen me over her in the final episode, she'd been gracious. Amazingly gracious. Strangely gracious. I'd thought for sure he'd pick her. They even *looked* good together.

But he chose *me*.

And I was okay with that. Actually more than okay. I figured I'd learn to love him. He was a good catch.

"We have some special champers just for this toast." She hustled as fast as her pink ruffles and four-inch heels would allow, over to a sweaty ice bucket, and returned with two bottles of what qualified as the 'good stuff.'

She gestured toward the bottle Lady held in her hands. "We can't toast this gorgeous bride with *that* crap."

Lady rolled her eyes, and I gave her my discrete 'I'm with ya, sister' half-smile. I planned to blow off these bitches—the bridesmaids *I had not chosen*—the moment the wedding was over. T minus forty-five minutes.

Except, of course, Lady.

"Mmmm. I just love *Dom*," she purred, smacking her lips after everyone had gotten a small pour. "Don't you, Alessia? I mean, I'm sure you and Mont have it all the time."

I didn't even know what *Dom* was. But I wasn't telling her that.

"Totally, Vanessa," I said, lying through my expensive, veneered smile.

"Ugh. Would someone answer that ringing cell?" another beauty from across the room whined.

"That is getting annoying," I said. "Whose phone is it?"

My question kicked off a flurry of activity, and the bridesmaids ran to search among the pile of purses on the bed.

"Here it is," one of them cried.

She ran over and handed me my crystal-encrusted Judith Lieber *minaudiere*, a kitschy replica of a tiny wedding bouquet.

Apparently, the stylist had thought carrying a real bouquet was not sufficient and that my purse needed to look like one, too.

"Better answer it quick. What if Mont's backing out?"

The room erupted in peals of laughter.

I sent the call to voicemail, but as soon as I did, it rang again. So, I turned off the ringer and threw it back in my bag. Then, the damn thing started to vibrate against the walls of my purse, making more noise than if it were actually ringing out loud.

For Christ's sake. I was supposed to walk down the aisle momentarily. Who could be calling? Wasn't everyone I knew already in the church, or at least, on their way?

I scooted over to the corner of the bride's waiting room for privacy and swiped my phone open.

"LeeLee?" I asked when I saw the name on the phone's screen.

"*Ohthankgod*, Alessia. So glad you finally answered."

I took a long, slow breath. The bustier must have succeeded in compressing my ribs, because I was actually, sort of, getting used to it.

"LeeLee, I'm about to get married. So, it's not the best time to be calling me, you know what I mean?"

"Okay. Okay. I tell ya what. I can't make it to the wedding—"

She was telling me this *now*?

"—but I'm out front with your wedding gift. Can you come outside real quick?"

She'd been on *Mates,* as those of us on the dating show called it, but had been eliminated early on, which had been a bummer, at least for me. She was one of the few cool girls in the group.

"LeeLee, are you kidding?" I looked at the time on my phone. "Mont's gonna pull up any minute in his limo, and the church is full of cameras. Can't you come back here? I'm in the bridal room hangout."

"Look, Alessia, just come out front. I'll make it really quick. I just want to give you your present in person. It's really very special."

I turned to find all the bridesmaids taking pictures of each other with their phones, then making the stylist take pictures of them altogether, posing and looking stunning, just like they'd taught us during the *Mates'* pre-show 'charm school,' as I called it. Yup, they coached us on how to walk and talk, gave us makeovers, and had us in the gym for several hours a day.

7

All this before the show even started taping.

My bestie Lady stood off to the side with the fakest damn smile I'd ever seen her wear, and the girls squealed over every photo they uploaded to their Instagram feeds.

That was another part of the *Mates* indoctrination. As stars of such a popular TV reality show, we were all considered to be 'influencers.' We were required to post all day, every day, until the terms of our contract were over.

Yes, reality TV stars got paid. And if you 'won,' like I did, you got paid a lot. In fact, I was due five hundred thousand dollars as the show's winner. Mont was due the same.

That's right. Between the two of us, we'd have a million fucking dollars.

Don't get me wrong. I wasn't doing this only for the money. Mont was a great guy, of which everyone constantly reminded me. I was lucky he'd chosen me. And now we were getting married in an all-expenses-paid five-star wedding courtesy of the network that produced *Mates*. They were making a killing on the show. Guess they had money to spare.

Which was fine by me.

"Okay, LeeLee. I'm gonna run out to the front of the church. You'd better be right there." I dropped my phone back in my *minaudiere* and hooked the little bag around my wrist.

I turned to the bridesmaids. They were so busy making sure their perfect faces were on Instagram I doubted they'd even notice me gone. But I played nice. "Ladies," I shouted over their racket. "I'm stepping out front really quick… to check my makeup in the daylight."

"Nooooo!" they all screamed.

"What if Mont sees you?"

"What if you trip and mess up your dress?"

"What if the press sneak a picture of you online before you've even started your walk down the aisle?"

I waved my hand to comfort everyone. "I'll be right back."

Before they could protest further, I dashed out the door.

The vestibule of the church was cool and much quieter than I thought it would be. I mean, just before a wedding, aren't people usually milling around, socializing, getting psyched for the big event?

"Alessia," a voice hissed from a dark corner of the church lobby, where songbooks were stored on a rolling bookcase.

"LeeLee, why are you hiding?"

"C'mere, Alessia," she beckoned, frantically waving her hand.

Why couldn't her wedding gift just be mailed, like everyone else's?

She held a door open that exited the side of the church, and we stepped outside. The sunlight was blinding after having been indoors for so long, and I squinted, my hand shielding my eyes.

Do not mess up the makeup.

She smiled broadly, looking me up and down in approval. "You look so amazing. Wow. Great rack." She pointed to my boob shelf.

"Thanks, LeeLee. Hey, I really gotta get back inside— "

And don't you know, as I peered around from the side of the church where LeeLee and I were sort-of hiding, Mont's limo pulled right up.

"Shit. Mont's here!" I hissed, ducking back behind the corner of the church.

My phone began to vibrate with a call from the bridesmaids, so I pulled it out of my bag, and this time, *really* turned it off.

I had to say, Montgomery Langton, my husband-to-be, was quite stunning in his simple tuxedo.

"He really is one good-looking guy, isn't he?" LeeLee breathed.

Seriously.

"So, hey, why'd you want to see me?" It seemed a little grubby to ask for my gift and run off, but I had a schedule to keep.

"Right," she said, as if she'd forgotten why she needed so desperately to see me moments before I was to walk down the aisle. She rummaged through her canvas cross-body bag and pulled out a large envelope.

A cash gift? I had no problem with that, even though most people just sent checks.

"Thank you, LeeLee. I'm sorry you can't make it."

And why couldn't she? Who cancels at the last minute but takes the time to drop off a gift?

"Yeah… it should be a good one. Hey, looks like Mont's inside so I'm gonna scoot off. See ya," she said breezily.

I watched her dart for her car as if she were under fire.

Strange, that one.

I peeked in the envelope, expecting to see the usual wedding card that said *Alessia and Montgomery* on the front.

But that's not what I saw. Nope, the wedding gift LeeLee had brought me was about the last thing in the world I expected to receive.

The envelope floated to the ground, landing half on the skirt of my wedding dress and half on the sidewalk. Seconds later, its contents joined the envelope on the ground, along with a couple of the big, fat tears that were running down my face.

Images of my handsome husband-to-be stared back, laughing at me, goading me, and mocking me. In one photo, his pants were around his ankles. One of the girls from *Mates*—actually, my bridesmaid Vanessa of the fancy champagne tastes—was on her knees. And yes folks, she was deep-throating my man.

In the other photo, said bridesmaid was bent over while Mont fucked her from behind.

And as if that shit weren't bad enough, they both wore blissful smiles as they twisted to face each other.

They were holding hands, too.

Mont never held my hand when we had sex.

He never looked at me so lovingly, either.

CHAPTER 2

DASH

It was a long-ass drive from Vegas back to Savage Mountain, a trek I made a few times a year for meetings, conventions, and just to have some fun. But, it never failed—on the drive home, I'd find myself wondering why the hell I'd taken on such a long road trip. To stave off my boredom, I popped a handful of peanut M&M's in my mouth. I was a sucker for those babies.

Gripes about the long drive aside, I was pleased with the good contacts I'd made at the hacker conference where I'd learned some new white hat—as well as black hat—moves. I couldn't wait to put them in motion and see if I got the results my fellow hackers claimed to be getting. You never knew about these guys, like who was on the up-and-up and who was full of shit.

Hacker conventions were funny that way. Everyone *claimed* to be white hat—another word for 'one of the good guys.' Like Robin Hood—perhaps a thief on the surface, but really a do-gooder in the final analysis.

Like me. I was a white hat hacker.

But I know not everyone there was. The black hat guys blended in with the rest of us, but they were the ones who exploited their technical prowess to their own—and usually no one else's—benefit.

They were the ones who made the rest of us look bad. In fact, they were the ones who hacked into my parents' savings account when I was a teenager and wiped out all their money.

They were the ones who convinced me that I'd study computer science, too, and I'd become twice the hacker any of them were. I planned to keep innocent people like my parents out of hacker reaches. It was the best revenge I could conceive of.

Put the fuckers out of business.

That's why I buddied up to them whenever I could. Keep your enemies close… and all that.

I couldn't stomach another M&M. Time for real food, and there was a small town up ahead with a tavern.

A disinterested waitress plopped a cheeseburger in front of me, and after two or three bites, I was pretty much done. I wasn't really even hungry, having stopped mostly out of boredom and to stretch my legs. I ordered a coffee to stall leaving and began doing a little recon via my phone on some of the hacker dudes I'd met at the con.

Some of these guys were legit, some were not, and some were strictly bad news. I always wondered why the worst of them even showed up. You never knew what kind of undercover law enforcement would be there. I supposed risk was part of the fun for them and gave them something to brag about later.

But a commotion at the bar kept dragging my attention from my work. As a rule, I minded my own business and didn't get involved in other peoples' crap, and the scene playing out just then threatened to become a shit show. Time to high tail it out.

Problem was, my waitress was busy gabbing on her cell in the kitchen doorway, not even bothering to hide her slack-ass attitude. So, I could either patiently wait for my check or just start walking toward the door to see if she woke up and remembered she was at work, and had a customer who wanted to pay.

But before I did either, a shriek came from the direction of the bar and aforementioned shit show.

Damn. I hadn't escaped in time.

I kid you not—there was a woman at the bar in a

wedding dress. One of those over-the-top monstrosities with a bottom that billowed out like a dangerous fire hazard and a top so tight her tits were about to spill out.

And she did not look happy.

'Course I had nothing to compare her to, since you didn't see many brides hanging out alone in bars. I mean, in the history of brides and bars, had there ever been an instance of one hanging out because she had nothing better to do? I doubted it.

"I told you to *fuck off*," she screamed a little unsteadily to a couple creeps who wouldn't leave her alone.

Hmmm.

I approached them carefully. "Guys, I think the lady prefers to drink alone."

She whipped around, apparently shocked at my effort. And what a hot mess she was.

Don't get me wrong. She was fucking beautiful. Or she had been before she'd been hit by whatever freight train had taken her out and turned her into a puddle of tragic emotion. Her dark hair was gathered into some sort of bride-y hairdo, but a good bit of it had escaped its control and was pointing in several directions.

Her makeup was pooled in little black moons under her eyes, and there was a smudge of red lipstick running off the side of her deliciously full lips. But what really got me was the sadness in her otherwise amazing green eyes.

Yeah, she was not having her best day, and it was clearly being made worse by the guys who were on her case.

"C'mon baby," one of them cajoled. "Did ya get stood up at the altar?"

"Darlin', I'll marry ya. Let's go right now. We can be in Vegas in three hours flat."

Ordering another tequila, she ignored them, which really only served to egg them on. The bartender, who must have been related to the slacker waitress, couldn't have given a crap about the whole situation.

"Guys. I think our friend here wants you to leave her alone."

I was quickly running out of polite things to say. But if these jokers wanted to see me pissed, that was their problem.

"Why don't you fuck off, faggot?" one of them spat.

Okay. This clearly wasn't going to be a one-and-done. Damn. I needed to get back on the road.

"Miss, do you need some help?" I asked the woman.

What the hell was she doing there, anyway?

She nodded slowly, looking at the guys and then me.

"Whatcha gonna do about it, pretty boy?" the scrawny one asked.

Really? I had at least fifty pounds on each of these guys. They looked like little kids compared to me. Which made me realize I needed to take it easy on them. I wasn't about to get thrown in the slammer for beating the shit out of two dirtbag rednecks.

So, I proceeded slowly, just like my special ops training had taught me.

I grabbed each of the twits by the front of their shirts and lifted them until their feet barely touched the ground.

"I think it's time for you gentlemen to leave." I walked them toward the door, which I kicked open with my foot.

An approach like this, a 'soft' fight, was always a potentially dangerous one. The offenders could swing when my hands were full—never a good thing—or just completely back down, like I was guessing they probably would.

So, it must have been my lucky day because the fear that crossed their faces was worth the price of admission.

The moment I let go of their shirts, they looked at each other and hustled out of the place.

"Thank you." The bride tried tucking a stray hair back into her hairdo.

"No problem." I waived the waitress over for my check.

But the bride grabbed it when it came. "Here. Let me get it. I owe you."

She pulled a rolled-up wad of cash out of a bejeweled bag that looked like a wedding bouquet and threw a hundred-dollar bill on the bar.

"You really don't have to do that, miss."

She shrugged forlornly. "Happy to. I got a bag full of wedding cash. Gotta spend it on something."

She downed her shot and waved the bartender over for another.

I climbed onto a bar stool. "Did you drive here? Because I don't think you're in any shape to drive home."

She shook her head, loose hair flopping around her face. "Nah. The wedding limo dropped me here. It was as far as they were allowed to go."

"Well, how are you getting home?"

"Dunno," she mumbled. "Don't care."

"Do you need a ride somewhere?" I asked.

This time, she turned on her barstool and looked me up and down. "I suppose so."

The bartender returned with the woman's change, a pile of one's and five's. Sliding off her stool, she just left it there.

"Whatcha waiting for?" she asked, heading for the door.

No surprise, my passenger conked out the minute we hit the freeway, and before we'd discussed where I might take her. It would be a few hours before I hit a town of any decent size, so I figured I could let her snooze for a while. I'd find a little motel closer to civilization and send her on her way.

"Ugghhhh."

I didn't know such a pretty girl could make such an unappetizing sound.

"I think I'm gonna be sick!" She clambered for the window button, but in her panic, only succeeded in unlocking her door.

I screeched to a stop on the shoulder, but the woman—whose name I didn't even know—didn't move quite fast enough. She vomited down the front of her wedding dress just as she got the car door open. She fell to her knees in the dirt on the side of the road, thankfully taking her mess and horrible stench with her.

It was a bona fide disaster.

I walked around to her side of the car, where she sat in a pile of soiled wedding dress, holding her head in her hands. Then she reached behind her back and began undoing the ties on her dress.

"Um, miss, I'm not sure you should undress right here."

She stopped. "I know. I don't have anything else to put on. But I have to get out of this. I can't breathe."

She leaned back against the car and looked up at the sky. "Universe, why don't you just shit on me a little more, today? See how much I can take."

I went around to my trunk and rifled through my

duffel bag. "Here. I have a T-shirt and some sweats you can throw on."

"Oh, my god, thank you." She grabbed the clean clothes, pulled the T-shirt over her head, and undid the top of her dress, which fell into the dirt, and then pulled the sweats up and under her skirt, which she then pushed down to her ankles. She put her white high heels back on, the only remnant of her bridal gear aside from the weird purse she was carrying.

Instead of looking like a sad bride, she now looked like a sad homeless person.

Then, as if she hadn't already been full of enough surprises, she reached under her T-shirt and, wincing in pain, yanked a piece of caution tape off somewhere on her upper body and threw it on the ground.

"Fuck that shit," she said, throwing her bridal clothing in a pile which she knelt on and began tearing apart the way a wild animal tore apart a carcass.

"That must have been expensive," I said.

She looked up at me, squinting in the setting sun. "Yeah, it was. But I didn't pay for it. So who cares?" She stood, wiped her dusty hands on the T-shirt of mine she was wearing, and got back in the car.

I think if she'd had a book of matches, she would have set the whole mess on fire.

"So, where do you want to go? Where can I take you? There's probably a bus station in the next town that can take you home," I suggested.

She leaned her head against the window and shook

it. "No. Can't go home. There will be TV cameras all over the place."

"TV cameras? Who are you, anyway?"

Pulling her vibrating phone out of her bouquet bag, she said, "No one you want to know. Take my word for it."

CHAPTER 3

ALESSIA

More had happened in the last six months of my life than in the entire twenty-six years preceding it.

The morning things exploded into weirdness of epic proportions, I had dressed in my scratchy polyester work uniform, just like every other day. I'd tied the jaunty neckerchief we were required to wear in a little square knot at my neck, pulled my hair into a neat ponytail—another requirement—swiped on some lipstick, and hit the road for another day behind the counter of a shitty little car rental agency.

My job was mind-numbingly unchallenging. The only thing making it bearable was that we were usually insanely busy. And, my best friend worked there. The days went by so fast I'd forget to have lunch. But, I always made time to dish at least a little with Lady, even if we had to wait until after work.

When our shifts were done, we'd go to one of the airport hotel bars, depending on the special offer on a given night. Dollar beers, two-dollar screwdrivers, three-dollar cosmos—we weren't picky—we just wanted the bargain. We rotated through them all, finding cheap alcohol like the pros we were.

We even got the occasional freebie because we were in uniform. People would send us drinks like we were important or something.

No complaints, here.

On the nights Lady and I went out after work, which was often, we'd recap any of the nice-looking men who'd come through the agency during the day and judge them by the car they'd rented. The guys who got the family vans, we forgot about. Ditto for the guys who got the convertible Mustangs, Corvettes, or whatever 'fancy' car we had on the lot. They were just trying too hard.

But the men who drove off in the mellow but masculine SUVs? Now, those were the ones we remembered. And talked about. Sometimes, we even wrote down their names and addresses so we could Google them later.

Although, that was strictly against the rules.

But no one would ever find out we'd cyber stalked a

couple hotties. Besides, we'd forget about them when the next day's batch of men came through.

I don't mean to make it sound like everyone who rented a car looked like they walked off the pages of *GQ*. Most of them did *not*. But the ones who *did*—well, I'd be lying if I didn't admit they brightened our day.

Sometimes, they even chatted us up.

One nice-looking man asked Lady out for drinks, which she gladly accepted. But things quickly went south when, at the bar where they were having drinks, he gave her his room key and told her to meet him upstairs in ten minutes after he'd had the chance to say good night to his wife and kids over FaceTime.

Yeah, no.

Then there was the fateful day Billy Brent came in. With his Hollywood good looks—thick, styled hair, suntan, and giant phony smile, he acted like a hot shit. So, yeah, I flirted. Before he left my station—by the way, he'd rented a yellow Corvette—he slipped me his card with his supposed 'private number and email.'

Whatevs, dude. You lost me when you got the 'Vette. Those were douchebag cars, usually rented by old farts, and they broke down like crazy. In fact, they were the worst cars in our fleet, but the agency kept them around because fools paid a small fortune to rent them.

Guess it more than made up for the never-ending repairs.

I chucked Billy Brent's card, even if it did have his

personal contact info, because I just couldn't hang out with guys like him.

But the funny thing was, when he returned his car three days later, he specifically made sure to get in my line.

"Hello, Mr. Brent. I hope all went well with your rental."

He gave me a huge smile, showing off his Hollywood whites. If I wasn't mistaken, he was seriously checking me out.

He leaned onto the counter separating us, as if he had a big secret to share. I leaned a smidgeon closer, just to be polite.

He smelled good. Really good.

"Say, Alessia," he said, reading my nametag, "I'm the producer of a popular TV reality show that I think you'd be *great* on."

Interesting proposition. If that *was* a proposition.

Lady was in the next station over, helping a group of elderly ladies trying to get a mini-van for their girls' weekend. But she was also straining to listen me and Mr. Good-looking.

"Well, thank you, Mr. Brent. It's nice of you to consider me, but I'm not into camping in the woods or doing other survivalist types of things. Joe down at the other end of the counter might be, though. He's been to Nepal and stuff." I gestured in Joe's direction. He was trying to get someone to pay for a car they'd damaged.

Billy laughed, showing off his Chiclet teeth. "No,

no, no, Alessia. My show's a dating program. There's one guy and twenty women. The guy has to pick one, and they usually get married at the end."

Oh? Had I seen that show? Yes! And god was it totally stupid—

Even worse than the outdoor survival shows.

"*The Mating Game!*" we both said at the same time.

He threw his hands up in the air like he'd achieved a major victory. "Ha! I knew you were a fan. I can always pick 'em out of the crowd."

Thank god he wasn't a mind reader, too.

"Alessia, what do you say to joining next season's program? We are in desperate need of a girl-next-door type—just like you," he said brightly, as if he were paying me the biggest compliment of my life.

"Oh, I don't know, Mr. Brent—"

My manager suddenly appeared at my shoulder.

"Mr. Brent, is everything okay?" she asked.

That was code for *if you don't need anything else, please hit the road.*

The line *was* getting pretty long.

"Well, hello," he said to her.

My manager, Selma, brightened immediately. God only knew the last time someone had flirted with her.

She coquettishly extended her hand. "Pleased to meet you, Mr. Brent. I am Selma Smith. *Manager.*"

"Miss—or is it *Mrs.*—Smith? I was just talking to your lovely associate, Alessia, about coming on my show. My TV show," Billy Brent said.

As if Selma were my agent, she pursed her lips. "Really? How do we know this would be a good move for our girl, here?"

She placed an arm around my shoulder, never mind that she was about the coldest person I'd ever known and that the line of customers was beginning to snake out the door, too.

"Well, Selma. This could be a very lucrative move for Alessia. Not to mention all the publicity that would be generated for your franchise *right here*." He thumped his forefinger on the counter for emphasis.

And that was all she wrote.

Selma was sold. "Let's all go back to my office and chat."

On the first episode of the show, they made me wear my uniform, pretending I'd just gotten off work and had to rush over to the giant mansion where all twenty of us girls were to live for the next few weeks. The rest of the women were all glammed up in evening attire.

That was my first clue that reality TV was not very real.

It quickly became apparent I was the token 'plain girl.' I was okay with that, though. I mean, I was getting paid fifty thousand dollars for doing not much of anything.

Well, I actually had to do a good deal before

shooting started. The list was long—I had to work out with a trainer, get my teeth fixed, lose eleven pounds, and get all the brassy highlights in my hair removed. But hey, it was all free, so who was I to complain? At least I had a couple months off from renting Corvettes to douche-y men trying to look cool.

Speaking of being away from work, Thelma, bless her heart, had given me all the time off I needed, so long as I mentioned the rental agency as often as I could without seeming too obvious. I explained to her that the show had a national audience and that she had only one location, but she didn't care.

For some reason no one knew, Bill Brent had taken a liking to me. Not a romantic or get-in-my-pants kind of liking, but more of a Pygmalion project kind of liking. As if he'd found me in a gutter or something and was leading me to a new, better life.

I hadn't known my situation before *Mates* was such shit, but okay.

All I knew was I had to look my best when we were shooting, get along with the other girls even though they were bitchy and gossiped behind each other's backs, and post lots and lots of selfies and other photos to Instagram. I was daily reminded that I was an 'influencer.' Not sure who I was influencing or what I was influencing them to do, but it was an easy job that took only a few minutes a day.

Of course, some of the girls acted like it was a full-time job.

At the end of the hour-long show each week, two or three girls were 'eliminated' by Mont, the lucky bachelor with his pick of twenty women. Those booted off usually cried their hearts out for the camera, and then as soon as shooting stopped, packed their shit and hightailed it out, happy to take with them whatever dough and free dresses they'd earned.

And if I were not mistaken, most of them were glad as hell to be freed from the cheesy show itself, the smarmy producer and host Billy, and his suck-up staff. Mont wasn't all that bad, though. He was a nice enough guy, and handsome, in a boyish but hot Doogie Howser sort of way.

Weeks later, the final show rolled around, and for some inexplicable reason, I was still in the running. It made absolutely no sense. The other girls were beautiful, worldly, and most of all, *really* wanted Mont and the five hundred thousand dollars they'd get if he chose them in the end.

I actually felt a little guilty that they were eliminated and not me, especially when they wanted so desperately to be *the one*.

During the final scene of the final show, which had seemed forever in coming, my name was called. Such a relief. Done at last! I could go back home with some money, a new wardrobe, a toned physique, and get on with my life. Go back to school. Something like that.

I walked off-camera and back to the table where they kept snacks and things for the cast and crew. I picked up a big strawberry cupcake, something I'd not had in ages because of my dieting, and sank my teeth into the sugary sweet when someone grabbed my arm and pulled me back on camera. The partially eaten cupcake was still in my hand, and the frosting was all over my mouth.

The other girl I'd been up against, Vanessa, the one whom I'd thought had been chosen, was off in a corner crying. Turned out he had *chosen* me, not *eliminated* me.

My bad.

Mont looked at me while Billy, off-camera, gestured for me to smile. But I had a mouthful of cupcake.

No matter. Mont got down on one knee and asked me to marry him.

My cupcake plummeted to the floor. Frosting side down.

CHAPTER 4

FORREST

"Yes, I agree. It's time to be tough and decisive," I said over secure video.

I wished to god I hadn't agreed to the video portion of the call. Audio would have been perfectly sufficient for what we were trying to accomplish. But with video, I couldn't yawn, rolled my eyes, or even stretch. No, it was imperative to remain professional at all times in my line of work, especially when negotiating the terms of a mission.

"For this to go forward, gentlemen, we require all funds be deposited in an offshore account, paid through an LLC. If that's amenable to you—"

What?

A woman had just passed by my office door. In a place I lived with four guys. On a remote mountaintop.

"Excuse me, we'll have to continue this call later." I clicked on the screen, and the men I'd been speaking with disappeared into blackness.

I lived surrounded by a security system that would rival Fort Knox's.

For good reason.

"Excuse me. Excuse me," I said, sprinting to catch up with the visitor who'd just about given me a heart attack.

We didn't do visitors on Savage Mountain, and certainly not unannounced ones.

"Oh, hi. I'm Alessia." A beautiful brunette with glittering green eyes turned to me and extended her hand cheerfully.

Out of the many strange things about her being there, the first one that struck me was that she was wearing sweats—and guys' sweats, at that. And she was swimming in them.

What the fucking fuck?

"Um, Alessia, what are you doing here? How'd you get up here, to the mountain?" I forced myself to keep calm, but my mouth was dry as a bone.

"Dan brought me. In his truck." She smiled brightly, like she got rides to the mountains all the time. No big deal.

But it was a big deal. A fucking big deal.

And my mouth grew drier still. I hadn't talked to a beautiful woman in far too long.

Regardless, she was not supposed to be there. Something had gone wrong. Very wrong.

I put my hand on the firearm hidden at my waist. "Who is Dan?"

I lived on Savage Mountain with three other guys, and not one of them was named Dan.

Confusion crossed her face, and she seemed so innocent, unlike any intruder I'd ever seen. "You know, Dan. He lives here. You don't know who I'm talking about? He was driving home from a convention in Vegas."

I frowned.

"You know, about six feet tall, almond shaped eyes, long-ish black hair."

Oh, Jesus.

"Do you mean *Dash*?"

Her hand flew to her head. "Yes, yes, yes. Sorry! In all the excitement, I forgot the poor guy's name. Dash. Yeah, Dash brought me."

"And how did Dash come to bring you here?"

Where was Dash, anyway?

She sighed. "Well. It's a long story. But the short version is he sort of picked me up in a bar. I'd had too much to drink."

I was going to kill him. That's all there was to it.

She put her hands on hips. "Great place you have here."

Right.

"Okay, Alessia. Let me show you to the kitchen. If you could hang out there a few minutes, I need to find Dash and have a chat with him."

She headed back in the direction she'd come from. "Oh, I know where the kitchen is. I'll head back there. Hey, do you mind if I grab a Coke? I noticed you had some in the fridge. I wanted to ask first," she said with a big smile.

She knew where the kitchen was? She'd been in our fridge? Jesus fucking Christ.

"DASH!" I hollered loud enough to be heard throughout the house.

He came running around the corner, passing Alessia on the way, and greeting her with a high-five.

Was I in *Twilight Zone* or something? Because it sure felt like it.

We left the smiling Alessia in the kitchen sipping her Coke.

"Dash," I said, ushering him into my office and slamming the door. "*Who* is that woman? Wait, no, I don't care who she is. What I really want to know is *why* she is here and *when* she is leaving."

He put his hands in his pockets and nodded slowly. "Yeah, I know I shouldn't have brought her. But she'd just left some guy at the altar and gotten drunk in a bar, so I gave her a ride. When I tried to let her off at a motel, she was crying so hard, I offered to bring her up to the house for a couple days. Just couldn't leave her."

"Are those your clothes she's wearing?"

He shrugged. "Yup."

I was speechless. Utterly.

He scratched his chin as if he were only just now thinking through the implications of bringing someone to the cabin. "Yeah, should have cleared it with you guys first, huh?"

I left Dash standing there and tracked down Turk and Remy, the other guys we lived with.

"Hey. Were you two aware Dash brought a woman here?"

Turk didn't look up from his computer. "Are you sure it's not just a blow-up doll?" He slammed his hand on the arm of his chair and threw his head back for a hard laugh at his own joke.

"Shut up, Turk," I said. "Remy, do you know what's going on?"

He frowned. "What do you mean he brought a woman here? Like to the mountain? Like a real one? With tits 'n stuff?"

I leaned toward them, raising my voice. "Yeah, he brought a woman to the mountain. To our house. She's real, and yes, she has tits. She's in the kitchen right now, having a Coke."

"No shit, man," Turk said, finally looking up at me.

I leaned my head out the door. "DASH!" I hollered

He ran in to join us, alarmed. "For Christ's sake, Forrest. Why do you keep screaming?"

Remy stood and walked toward Dash, his hands

held out. "Dude, what's up with your bringing someone up here?"

Dash ran his hand through the dark hair that hung to his shoulders. "Oh, man. What a story I have for you guys."

He got comfortable in an office chair and proceeded to tell us how he'd come upon Alessia.

I couldn't believe what I was hearing.

"What made you think, for one minute, Dash, that it was okay to bring someone here?"

I took a deep breath. "You know security is our top priority. All the years we've lived here, we've not brought a single person around without extensive advance planning."

He nodded guiltily, still not getting the severity of my ire. "Yeah. You're right. But I couldn't leave her. I mean, what a fucked up situation. She was bawling so hard, I just blurted out, *come stay with us for a couple days.*"

Remy frowned. At least *he* understood the signifi-cance of the situation. "Why can't she just go to her own home?"

Turk just sat back, taking it all in.

Dash leaned forward, elbows on his knees. "I guess there are cameras from a reality TV show trying to track her down or something. It really is a shitty situa-tion. But hey, she's hot, isn't she? I mean, that ass and that rack. You should have seen her in her wedding dress. Cripes."

Once again, Dash was thinking with his little head. Which had gotten him into trouble before.

"Guys," he continued, not ready to give up, "c'mon. You can see she's harmless. I mean, she's just sweet as could be."

I took a deep breath and looked up at the ceiling.

He gestured toward Remy and Turk. "Come meet her. You'll like her. I know you will"

"Nice to meet all of you." Alessia cheerfully shook everyone's hand like it was her first day at a new job.

And now that I had a bit of distance from her, I was able to really appreciate how pretty she really was. I could see that under her sweats she had a banging body —nice round hips and full breasts.

Although she wore white high heels with Dash's sweats.

Bizarre.

She caught me looking at her. "Hey. Forrest, I know these duds look terrible. Dash loaned them to me after I puked all over my wedding dress. Well, except for the shoes." She pointed to her feet, as if I hadn't noticed.

"Where's the dress now?" Turk asked.

She shrugged. "Side of the road somewhere. Not sure where we were when we pulled over. But I destroyed it. Left it in shreds. You should have seen me."

She mimed tearing something apart with great satisfaction and then touched her temple as if she'd just thought of something important. "Hey, I was wondering if you had any stores nearby. Where I could, you know, get some clothes and toiletries? Stuff like that."

Fuck. Did that mean she expected to stick around, because that simply was not an option. But I wasn't about to lower the boom on her until I talked to the guys. Get everyone on the same page. Come up with an exit plan. Literally.

"I'll take you to town later so you can pick up some things," Turk volunteered.

He'd take her to town later so she could find a hotel and stay there. And never come back.

"Alessia, why don't you take a walk on the property? It's really beautiful. The guys and I were about to have a meeting, anyway."

Their heads snapped in my direction.

"We were? What for?" Remy asked.

So much for subtlety.

Alessia looked out the window and nodded. "Good idea, I'll get some fresh air. So beautiful here."

When she was gone, I turned to Dash.

"Dude, you are fucking kidding, bringing a reality TV star here? What are you gonna do when the TV cameras show up? Pretend we're running a summer camp?" I asked, pacing. I pointed a finger at him. "You brought her up here. You need to tell her she can't stay."

"Really, Forrest? Do you have to be such a dick? The girl needs help."

Yeah, I guess I was a dick for protecting all we'd worked so hard for. For building a sanctuary for us to retreat to when we were between our private security missions. A place where our enemies—and there were a lot of them—were unlikely to ever find us.

"So, help me, Dash, if you fuck all this up—"

"What, Forrest?" he snapped, getting in my face. "What will you do?"

Remy dashed over with his hands up like a *stop sign*. "Guys, guys. Let's discuss this calmly. Dash shouldn't have brought her, but the fact is, she's here right now. I propose we let her stay a couple days and then drop her at the hotel of her choice. *Adios*, baby. Tell her to forget she ever knew us, or the consequences could be dire."

Dash whipped around to Remy. "Oh, so now you're going to threaten her life? Nice. Really nice," he growled.

Remy was right. Not ideal, but sometimes, threats were the only way to get your point across.

CHAPTER 5

ALESSIA

I nearly fainted when I saw all four guys in one room together. I mean, what gorgeous examples of pure, manly, righteousness. It was incredible men like that existed, never mind actually lived together.

With no women around. At least that I could see.

And yet, from what I *had* seen, they were very different from each other. Probably what made their weird mountain-living arrangement work.

As I'd been instructed, I wandered, as best I could in my wedding shoes, around the grounds surrounding the 'cabin,' which was really like a high-end resort with rustic-but-not-too-rustic details. Some cool, old, rusty logging equipment sat in the corner of the yard that gave the place character, but not so much it looked like a Disney theme ride.

And I had to say, the grounds were amazing in a wild landscape sort of way. It was clear someone maintained the place, but not to the extent it looked like an overly manicured hotel property. It was the kind of yard I'd always wanted.

The guys had good taste in decorating, I had to hand them that. Even if they preferred to live in the middle of bumfuck nowhere.

When I thought about it, I actually had no idea where I was—I'd fallen asleep for the last couple hours of the drive and missed any and all landmarks. I could be on the moon, for all I knew.

My cell connection was iffy, at best—because mountains, of course—so Google Maps was not of any use. That left me at the guys' mercy, but—I really had no sense of unease about it. Go figure.

They seemed cool. I mean, the Forrest guy was kind of harsh and bossy, in wicked contrast to his dimples and sandy blond hair. But then, he did have one of those neck tattoos, so I guess that buys you entry into the bad boy's club.

But the others—Dash, Turk, and Remy—were nice enough. No complaints there, and they were certainly easy on the eyes.

Regardless, my overall opinion of men at the moment was not too terribly positive. In fact, it was at an all-time low given the masterful fucking-over Mont had dealt me.

To be honest, I'd been pressured into marrying him. I liked him just fine—I figured I'd eventually love him. We'd had lots of fun dating during the show and even when the cameras were off us—but, if I had my way, I would have liked to just date him for a while, out of view of the public and, of course, the *Mates* TV show. But for a variety of reasons, that was not possible.

I know ratings and all that other TV crap played a roll in how things came together. The show had wanted us to get married while their viewing audience was still interested. Something about if they waited too long, everyone would forget about us. Strike while the iron is hot.

I'd really been ready to get out of the fishbowl exis-tence of a reality TV contestant. The constant coverage of our lives was a major pain in the ass for all of us on the show, except for the occasional psycho girl who was desperate for attention. I mean, everyone who left the show after being eliminated, after a fake-ass on-camera broken hearted cry, pretty much bolted from the house.

I wondered on more than one occasion if *they* weren't the real winners.

But I guess when you're a network and you're supposed to produce material that makes money, letting love take its course is too much of a wild card.

Yet Mont had pursued me. Everyone told me how

lucky I was he'd chosen me that, after a while, I guess I believed it. But if he loved me, he sure had a funny way of showing it.

Like by fucking Vanessa.

What Dash didn't know, because I was too humiliated to tell him, was that when he dropped me at the motel after he'd picked me up in that dive bar, I'd gone into reception to book a room, and my credit card had been declined. Sure, I had enough cash to get by for a while, but I was so blown out that Mont had cancelled my card, I lost my shit.

Unfortunately for Dash, he was waiting out front in his truck and was the one to catch me when I realized just how badly I'd been fucked over. He'd thought I was just generally sad, which I was, but he didn't know the card cancellation pretty much told me all I needed to know.

Montgomery Langton didn't give a shit about me, and he never had.

So, that was not the best day.

But what the hell was I doing in the mountains with a bunch of guys who talked about 'missions' and 'special ops,' whatever those were? I mean, were the four of them criminals? What did criminals look like anyway?

I hoped I wouldn't be there long enough to learn any more than I already had because I didn't want to know anything else. I wanted only to get home and get on with my life, out of the glare of TV cameras. Which might not be so easy.

Never had my work at the car rental agency, wearing my sweaty polyester uniform, looked so appealing.

My intermittent cell coverage showed the non-stop calls I'd been missing, mostly from people more concerned about their paychecks drying up than with me. Sure, my BFF Lady had called, but so had a slew of other people, like Billy the smarmy producer, and my half sisters, who'd had their hands out since they heard how much money I stood to earn.

When I'd agreed to go on *The Mating Game*, they'd told me I was crazy and it was the stupidest thing they'd ever heard of.

Until they learned the show's winner would walk away with half a million dollars.

Yup, that's when they started being really nice to me and taking an interest in my otherwise uninteresting life.

There were texts, phone calls, emails, and lots of compliments on how I looked on the show.

They were very curious about whether I got to keep all the clothes I wore. And what size they were.

I'm surprised they didn't back up to the *Mates* house with a U-Haul to cart away whatever they could get their hands on.

But since I'd run out on Mont? Let's just say they weren't pleased.

After a couple frantic text messages to confirm I had indeed robbed them of any winnings they might have been able to extort from me, the communications came to an abrupt stop. It was like I didn't exist any longer.

You know who *hadn't* called me? Mont.

No surprise there, I guess.

So, while I was outside the cabin and my phone had a few bars, I reached out to Lady. She picked up on the first ring.

"Girl, what the fuck!" she screamed.

"Ack. You hurt my ears," I said.

"I haven't heard from you since you sent that text that you were bugging out. What was I supposed to think? I didn't know whether you were dead or alive."

"C'mon, Lady. I'd tell you if I were dead."

Silence.

"Alessia, that doesn't make any sense—"

"Okay, I know. Look, I'm sorry I worried you. I'm staying… um, at a cabin. In the mountains."

She gasped. "*What* cabin? *What* mountains?"

"To be honest, I'm not sure. But there are four guys here who are super nice—"

"You're with *strangers*? Have you lost your mind?" she shrieked.

"Lady, it's not really like that—"

"You know, Alessia, I've been worried sick about you. Seriously. Like I thought you might be dead or something."

"I'm really sorry—"

"On top of that, you haven't been around to deal

with the fallout of all this bullshit. As your official BFF, everyone seems to think I know every last detail of your life, including why you left Mont at the altar, and where you are now. Seriously, I've had reporters knock on my door. *My door!*"

Oh. I hadn't considered the world would see Lady as my wingwoman. Which she kind of was.

"I'm sorry about that. I hadn't realized—"

"Alessia, please tell me why that creep Billy Brent, the producer of your show, is so hell-bent on finding you. Is there something going on that you want to tell me?" she asked.

"Well, I guess they're upset I didn't marry Mont. I spoiled their show or something."

I could hear her pacing. "But I overheard him calling you his 'ace in the hole.' What does that mean?"

Interesting.

"I think that meant, Lady, that his show would be way more successful with me than without. That they wanted to show the plain girl next door could be swept off her feet by the handsome prince."

Apparently, they'd wanted to tell that story so badly, they didn't care that Mont had another woman he was far more interested in.

"Alessia, I heard him say one more thing I need to tell you."

"What is that?"

"Well, I'm sure it was just a figure of speech, but it

was disturbing. He said that if you ruined his career that he'd... he'd kill you."

What?

She continued. "I'm sure he didn't mean it, and that he was just angry, but it seemed so over the top." She paused. "Could it have to do with the fact that they paid for everything? All the wedding stuff? Do you have to pay them back?"

Cripes. It hadn't even occurred to me whether I was going to be stuck with the bill for that fiasco.

Screw them. I'm sure by now they'd seen the photos of Mont fucking someone else. Surely, they'd understand I couldn't go through with the wedding.

Right?

"You know what I'm gonna do, Lady?" I asked. "I'm going to call Billy. See what he has to say. Don't tell anyone you heard from me. If anyone asks anything, play dumb."

She sighed loudly. "All right. But just keep me posted so I don't have to worry."

"Promise." I swiped the phone closed.

I was thankful I'd found the one spot on Savage Mountain where my phone worked. I didn't budge while I dialed Billy Brent, *The Mating Game's* creator, host, and producer.

"Is that you, Alessia?" he asked before he even said hello.

Actually, he wasn't *going* to say hello.

"Yup, it is, Billy."

He exhaled loudly. "You know what position you've put the network in with your shenanigans? I hope you have plans to get your ass back to town so we can finish the show like it says in the contract you signed." As he spoke, his words got louder and louder until he was screaming.

I didn't like being screamed at. I mean, no one did. But for some reason, it terrified me. Left me frozen in place.

Except that at that moment, I was pissed. And Billy was about to be on the receiving end of it. All of it.

"Billy," I said slowly, "did you know Mont was fucking some other woman?"

"Um… well… Alessia, that has nothing to do with your contractual obligations to the show."

He did not just say that.

"Really? You pressured me into marrying someone who was involved with another woman? And why did you do that, Billy?" I clenched my teeth until they hurt.

"Look, Alessia, I know this is probably hard for you to understand, but this is business, plain and simple. *The Mating Game* must make money, and in order for it to make money, it has to be popular. It needs viewers. Lots of them. We're competing with hundreds of other things people can watch. So we have to give them something to keep coming back to. I mean, the public loves you, Alessia. You can't let your fans down."

Excuse me while I barf.

"Okay, Billy. So, you just admitted, in a roundabout

way, that you knew about Mont. Why'd he do it, then? Why'd he pretend to be in love with me, ask me to move in with him, and actually be willing to walk down the aisle with me?"

I could practically hear Billy rolling his eyes. "Alessia, you know how you were supposed to get half a million dollars if you won and finished the show?"

"Yeah."

Guess I'd flushed that down the drain.

"Well, if Montgomery convinced you to marry him, he was set to earn a million dollars."

Oh.

I sat down in the dirt right where I was standing. Actually, I didn't sit—it was more like my legs gave out under me.

I could barely speak, so I whispered. "Was the whole thing a set-up? Rigged? He was never interested in me?"

Silence.

"Billy, you and everyone else pressured me into marrying someone who didn't care about me?"

"Alessia. That's how reality shows work. It's about ratings. Not winning or losing. That stuff is all decided off-camera. Everyone wants to see the girl next door win. That's why we picked you and why you have to come back and finish things. Give your fans what they are dying for."

CHAPTER 6

TURK

"All right guys, take it down a notch. C'mon. We have work to do. Can't have you two at each others' throats."

"Fuck off, Turk," Forrest said, giving me one of his famous dirty looks and turning back to Dash.

Dash and Forrest had never been the best of friends. They respected each other, but their personal styles were vastly different. Dash, while hardly a wimp, was kind-hearted and wanted to help everyone and everything. You wouldn't believe some of the injured animals he brought home, which he successfully nursed back to health. Made me wonder if he should have been a vet.

Forrest, on the other hand, carried the weight of the world on his shoulders, and never let anyone forget it.

He was a perfect example of the fact that in our line of work, you leave behind what most would think of as a 'normal life.' Some of the things we've seen in the field and on our missions—well, they change you. They settle into your brain like a permanent fixture and crowd out some of the happier, lighter thoughts and memories that help most of us get through the day.

And for some of us, that change comes harder than for others. Like Forrest.

In fact, it wasn't that long ago I had to talk Forrest down off the ledge at the grocery store. Some dude cut him off in the checkout line, and next thing I knew, the unlucky bastard was in a headlock—not a fun place to be when Forrest was involved. I managed to separate the two and get Forrest the hell out of there before anyone called the cops.

The crazy thing was that as soon as he got to the car, he'd forgotten what had happened.

That's the consequence of committing extreme acts of violence against other human beings—for some, the slightest provocation shuts down the normal response and triggers the aggression of a warrior. It was both the biological and physiological price of the work we did, whether we were on a mission too dirty for the Army to take on or we'd been hired by a private company to carry out something highly secret and possibly even illegal in the country where we were working.

Dash and Forrest needed to keep their heads on straight. There was no room for any incidents or other drama at the cabin, especially because we were preparing for an important summit meeting with our business partners here on our property—a first for us.

We'd worked too long and too hard to mess things up now.

Most of us worked or went on mission only once or twice a year these days, and that was only if we really wanted to. We were compensated so well, that's all we needed to keep our nest eggs nice and feathered. I figured I could retire in a year or two and maybe go back to college or something. Do one of those online programs so I could stay up on the mountain in peace and quiet. The possibilities were endless, and I wanted to keep things that way.

I liked having options. And Forrest's hot head was not going to limit mine in any way.

Remy jumped in. "Yeah, guys, you gotta chill. In fact, I suggest we all take a break. Reconvene tomorrow or something." His calm nature always made him the voice of reason, which was why his work as a negotiator was in such high demand.

"Great idea, Remy," I said, stretching. "I told Alessia I'd take her into town, so maybe I'll do that now."

Forrest shook his head and slammed his hand on his desk. "I know you guys don't agree with me, but I think you should drop her at a hotel. She doesn't belong up here with us."

Dash smiled. "Even though she's pretty nice to look at?"

Forrest tried to suppress a smile. "Yeah, yeah. Okay, she *is* gorgeous."

"I see that you guys are still capable of thinking with your little heads," Remy said, amused.

Forrest laughed and cuffed him on the shoulder. "Yeah, well, fuck you too, dude."

"What do you think of Savage Mountain so far?" I asked Alessia as we drove to town.

She'd been lost in thought with her forehead pressed to the passenger side window, but she turned to me with her incredible smile.

"Oh, yeah. Beautiful. Just gorgeous. The house is insane. Although, I'm not sure we should be calling it a house. It's more like a crazy huge mountain mansion."

I laughed. "It is pretty damn nice. I love it, myself."

She looked back out the window. "It's so nice and quiet after living in the house with all those girls on *The Mating Game*. And those stupid TV cameras all over the place, sometimes even when we were sleeping. The only way to get privacy was to go to the bathroom."

"Are you glad you went on the show?"

She looked down at her chipped white polish and

sighed, shaking her head. "It was a mistake. A big mistake."

"Sorry to hear that." I pulled up to one of the town's few clothing stores.

Before getting out, she pulled a wallet out of her hoodie pocket and emptied it into her lap.

"Wow. Where'd you get all that cash?" I asked, watching her line up a bunch of twenties and a few hundreds.

"Mmmm. It's really not that much when you consider my now ex-fiancé turned off our joint credit card. This is the wedding gift money. I was going to take it on my honeymoon."

She placed her money, now organized, back in the wallet. "I suppose since the wedding was cancelled, the gifts should go back. But the cash, I'm keeping for my trouble."

"Do you have enough?" I asked.

If she needed some extra, well, it would be no skin off my back.

She shrugged. "I think so. I mean, I don't need a ton of things. Just some clothes for the couple days I'm up here. Then I'll go home and hopefully the press will have lost interest in the whole drama. I can go back to work and live in happy anonymity."

While I was glad to hear she only planned to crash at the cabin for a few days, it was also a little jarring. I mean, we didn't have women—especially women who looked like Alessia—on our property or even in our lives. She was making me remember what I was missing out on, given the life I'd chosen.

It was nice to have a woman to chat with, even if she did look like a homeless woman in Dash's clothes. A beautiful homeless woman.

She looked at me just before she jumped out. "I'll be fast. I know exactly what I want."

If she knew what she wanted, then why did she go on that ridiculous TV show?

Alessia wasn't as fast as she said she'd be, so I put a little change in the parking meter and took a walk up Main Street.

It snaked through the charming town at the base of Savage Mountain, a town we guys spent almost no time in. We were busy, and besides, preferred to keep low profiles. As long as we were working private security, our lives were not our own, and as long as we were basically warriors for hire, we were targets. We might be able to let up on our constant vigilance someday, but for now, we were on constant alert.

I grabbed a cup of coffee and ambled back to the car, where I thought Alessia might be waiting.

She was nowhere to be seen. And we needed to get back home.

Shit.

I looked up and down the street and headed for the store where I'd left her.

"Hello! Over here!"

I couldn't immediately identify the woman running toward me and yelling, but she was carrying several large shopping bags.

Then she got closer.

My eyes bugged open. "Holy shit. Is that you, Alessia?"

"Yeah," she said, twirling in a circle. "Look at me. I feel like a new woman. I'm wearing *normal* clothes again."

Yowsa. I was glad she felt good in her new clothes, because I seriously liked looking at her in them.

She wore a swingy little skirt and a short top showing off her flat stomach. She'd ditched Dash's too-big flip-flops for a pair of white sneakers.

Simply put, she was adorable.

A fact established by the twitch in my cock.

"Let me take those bags from you. Looks like you did some real damage."

She handed off her purchases. "Everything was on sale. Hey, I'm gonna run into the drugstore for some toiletries okay?"

I threw her bags in the back seat and watched her run across the street. Who knew she had such gorgeous legs under those baggy old sweats?

Alessia swiped her phone open on the drive back up the mountain.

"Well, if it isn't Billy Brent."

She'd finally answered after it had rung about fifty times. And it was a good thing, because I was considering throwing the damn thing out the window as I drove.

Clearly, this was a call from someone she'd been avoiding, and when she finally did answer, she looked at me and dramatically rolled her eyes.

"You can't just come get me. I'm not a prize that you fetch when you're ready. Besides," she said with satisfaction, "you have no idea where I am."

Shit. This Billy Brent guy thought he could drive up to the cabin? Just pop in?

Um, no.

That would not be good. Not for anyone.

"Alessia," I hissed, loudly enough to grab her attention but not be heard by her caller, "DO NOT have anyone come up here."

"Hold on, Billy," she said, putting the phone on *mute*.

"Sorry, Turk. What was that?"

"You don't want that guy coming to the cabin. In fact, you don't want anyone coming to the cabin. It will not end well."

It wouldn't end well for her, either, but I kept that to myself.

She nodded in agreement. "Don't worry, Turk. Even

if he *could* come up here, I wouldn't tell him where I was."

Smart girl.

She went back to her call. "No Billy, I'm not posting images of my *vacation* on Instagram. I'm not even on a vacation. I'm done with you and your whole show. You and Mont can go fuck yourselves."

Before she swiped her phone *closed*, a string of screamed expletives came over the line.

Unbothered, she dropped her phone in the backpack she'd just purchased and brushed her hands together as if she were wiping off dirt. "I hope he rots in hell."

"I take it he's from the show?" I asked.

"Yup. The producer and host. Major slime bag. Master manipulator. 'Course I got sucked in, so I'm to blame as well for the whole shit show that has become my life."

She turned and looked at me. "Um… is it a problem, my staying with you guys a couple days? I mean, I assumed it was okay, but I never really asked. That was actually really rude of me, wasn't it?"

I laughed. "Well, it looks like you're staying at least tonight since we're already headed back up."

She winced. "Ouch."

"Tell you what, I'll discuss it with the guys."

Her gaze snapped to the side of the road, and she twisted to look behind us.

"Oh my god! Pull over! Please!"

What the hell? I swerved to the small shoulder, my heart pounding.

"*Puppies!*" she screamed and jumped out of the car before I'd even fully stopped.

She nearly gave me a heart attack over *puppies*?

Okay, this woman was beautiful, but crazy as fuck, too.

In the rear view mirror, I watched her run back several yards on the side of the road. Someone had pulled over in their truck, set out a basket of puppies, and sat next to it in a folding lawn chair. And before I knew it, Alessia was back at the car.

Holding a squirming little puppy.

"Ohmygod, Turk. Isn't she the cutest? Do you think anyone would mind if I brought her back to the house? Just look at her!"

Um, yeah, the guys would mind.

But I didn't.

The joy on her face was too precious to risk. I knew all too well what a dog could mean when your life was in a rough spot.

"Get in," I told her. I couldn't say no to the woman.

I was in deep shit.

She squealed. "Thank you! What should we call her? Oh, my god, we need a really good name." She smothered the puppy's nose with kisses, and the little pooch licked her right back.

It was love at first sight for the two.

I pulled back onto the road. "Okay. When we get

back to the house, tell everyone it's my dog. Then they can get mad at me if they need to."

"Okay. Thank you, Turk!"

The little critter whined and then peed all over Alessia's new skirt.

Unfazed, she threw her head back and laughed with such pleasure, I felt pretty good about supporting her puppy acquisition.

"But I do have a serious question, Alessia. With all that you have going on in your life, you really want to take on a dog?"

Her face got serious. "I know," she said slowly, biting her lip in the cutest possible way.

Shit.

I took a deep breath. "I grew up in foster care," I blurted.

She turned to me, providing her full attention.

"I was lucky. I was with the same family nearly all my life, and they were good to me. But it was still traumatic, and sometimes, the only thing that kept me going was their family dog, who took a liking to me. He ended up really being *my* dog, at least until I left for the military."

"Wow."

"So, I know what that dog means to you. I'll make sure you can keep her at the house, for as long as you're with us."

Alessia screamed with delight so loudly, the puppy

howled. She reached over and kissed me on the cheek and squeezed my fingers as we approached the house.

She held the dog up and looked in her face. "Would you look at that, little puppy, things are looking up for the both of us."

It looked like things were looking up for all of us.

CHAPTER 7

ALESSIA

"Lady, you let Selma know I was coming back to work soon, right?" I lay back on my bed, where, interestingly, my phone worked just fine.

It was beyond me why I so eager to save a shitty little job in a shitty little car rental agency where I had to wear a shitty little uniform. Made no sense.

And yet, I was compelled to hang on to one of the few things in my life that felt stable. Dependable. Solid.

Unlike Mont, my fucking ex.

Lady laughed. "Yeah, I told her. Don't worry. Hey, I gotta tell you, there have been TV cameras hanging out here, waiting for you. Selma's freaking loving it. I mean, you'd think *she* was the reality TV star. She goes out there to talk to them, and then tells people to come rent a car from us. It's hilarious. She calls it free advertising. And, I think it has actually boosted business, if you can believe it."

I pictured our boss, Selma, an odd duck of a woman who'd made the rental office her life's work, tall and thin with her perfectly fitted and pressed uniform. Every single day.

We only got a couple uniforms, so Lady and I had always wondered how much time she must have spent caring for hers. Sure, I washed mine, but an iron had never touched them. And if the hem was falling down on my pants? I didn't mend it—I used a freaking stapler to hold it up.

But I couldn't complain about the woman. She was pretty nice to all of us and was so excited when I got on *Mates*. 'Course, she thought it could be good for business. Whether or not it was good for *me* was not so much of a consideration.

"How long do you think the cameras will be here? Won't they eventually lose interest?" Lady asked.

"God, I wish I knew. I'd think, at some point, they would. Or maybe another season will start and they'll be all over that cast. I'll be old news by then."

"So, what's it like there? With those guys?" Lady asked.

I looked around my bedroom, which was actually pretty nice, and tickled my puppy behind the ears.

Remy had found a leash for her in their shed, and I couldn't wait to get started on training her outside.

"The cabin is freaking gorgeous, Lady. You should see it. Really high ceilings and chandeliers made from animal horns. Dark wood floors covered in expensive oriental rugs, and heavy, overstuffed furniture with lots of pillows and soft throws. It's like a freaking hotel or something."

In any other situation, I'd be beyond thrilled to be there.

She sighed deeply. "It sounds like an awesome getaway."

I don't know if it was a getaway as much as a hideout.

"Well, you know what's best, Lady? The guys. You should see them. It's like they walked out of an issue of the Journal of Handsome Ruggedness. All four are so freaking hot—gorgeous and totally cut. Honestly, I can barely breathe when I look at them. But it doesn't matter. I won't be here long. In fact, they don't really want me here, anyway. I gotta figure out when to go home and get back to my old life."

"Well, I miss you, girl. Hurry back. Things aren't the same without you. Although, at least when you were on the show, I could turn on the TV and see you there. Now, I don't even get that."

"Ugh. Fuck that show. And all those people, especially Mont."

"I thought he really loved you. At least, it seemed like it on TV," she said.

I'd thought he'd loved me, too. Or if not that, at least he cared about me and liked me a lot.

But did I love him? That was a different question.

And the answer was no, not really.

I could have grown to love him. I *liked* him a lot and thought he was a good guy. My agreeing to marry him had made so many people happy that I thought it made me happy, too. And I guess it sort of had. We were both going to get paid a lot of money by the show, and I figured I probably wouldn't even have to go back to work.

So much for that.

Thank god I learned what I did before I'd walked down the aisle. And to think he'd been doing one of the dumb bitches who was in my goddamn wedding. Vanessa, good old Vanessa, who I thought was my friend. She'd helped me get my wedding dress on, for heaven's sake.

What an idiot I was.

Then Billy called me as soon as I was finished talking to Lady. He wouldn't leave me alone. Just when I was forgetting about my public humiliation, he'd beg me to come back as if just the day before we hadn't spoken, and I'd not told him he would never be coming to get me so I could go back on his show.

First of all, I didn't want to see him or anyone else from *The Mating Game*. But more importantly, if he did show up at the cabin, I was pretty sure he'd be chased off by gunfire.

While I didn't know anything about what the four guys did for work, one thing I *was* sure of was that they were not exactly welcoming to guests.

The only reason they let me stick around was that they felt sorry for me, I was pretty sure.

"Billy, why are you calling me again? I have not changed my mind, nor will I."

"Look, I got something to talk to you about, Alessia. I think you're gonna like what I have to say."

Always the salesman.

"Billy, I doubt anything you have to say would interest me. In fact, you need to quit calling me. I'm not coming back to your show. Ever. And in fact, when I do return to civilization, I may just let the press know how phony *The Mating Game* is."

I heard him suck in his breath. I'd clearly hit him where it hurt.

"Oh, Alessia. That's where you're wrong. Under the terms of your contract, you can't talk about the show in any way that disparages it."

"Yeah, right, Billy. I'll say whatever I want—"

Undeterred, he raised his voice. "What if I told you I could pay you more? A lot more?"

Oh.

"I tell ya what. First, pay me what you owe me. Then, we can talk about next steps," I said.

His voice got louder still. "No can do. You have not

fulfilled your contractual obligation. But you still have the chance to do that. You could come back and explain you got cold feet. Then you could beg on camera for Mont to forgive you. Then, and only then, will you be paid."

Did I hear that right?

"You know what Billy, you are a two-bit, low-level trash TV whore. And that's all you'll ever be."

"You bitch—"

I swiped my phone closed and this time, blocked his number.

"I thought that dog was Turk's," Remy said, noting how cozy the puppy and I were.

I took my seat at the breakfast table. "Oh. Well, she is. But I asked if I could take care of her for a few days. Try to train her a bit. Until I left, that is."

I looked at Turk for reinforcement.

Turk nodded. "Yeah. Alessia's taken a real liking to her. So, I don't mind if they hang out together."

Loved that guy.

"Yup. Hey, I'm gonna put her out on the front porch while we eat," I said.

"What are you going to name her?" Remy asked, looking at Turk.

He leaned back in his chair. "Not sure. Maybe Ozzy. After Ozzy Osbourne."

Wait a minute. Didn't I get to name my own dog?

"What do you think, Alessia?" Turk turned to me.

I forced a smile. "It's great."

What a stupid name for a dog.

As soon as breakfast was over, I brought 'Ozzy' back inside and she was treated to the morning's leftovers. She was so freaking happy, that her little butt wiggled back and forth while she chowed down on her food.

Even Forrest couldn't resist her. He crouched to pet her, cooing in a way I didn't think was possible for him.

Unfortunately, as soon as she got a look at who was stroking her, she pulled back, bared her teeth, and growled angrily.

I bit my tongue to keep from laughing.

"Christ." Forrest yanked his hand back.

What a little badass Ozzy was.

Remy laughed. "Ha, did you see that? Not even the dog likes Forrest!"

Forrest rolled his eyes. "Whatever."

"Alessia, what are you doing today?" Remy asked, finishing the last of the dishes.

Christ, this guy was good-looking. Sandy blond hair, goatee, prominent brow. He couldn't have been more handsome had Michelangelo sculpted him.

"I think I'll take Ozzy out for a nice walk."

"Great idea. Just don't go too far. We don't want you getting lost."

"I'll be careful," I called over my shoulder as Ozzy

and I left the house.

I didn't have to go far, not that I would have anyway, to find a nice patch of wildflowers. How pretty a small bunch of them would look in my room, maybe in a mason jar if I could swipe one from the kitchen. I gathered a nice handful while Ozzy rolled around.

Shit. What was that?

Ouch.

A goddamn bee stung me on my cheek, just below my eye.

Raising my hand to the pain, I brushed away the bee, which fell to the ground dead, and I scratched until I got the stinger out.

That's when it really started to hurt.

Ozzy and I hustled back to the house, and I grabbed some ice from the freezer.

"Where ya going?" Turk called from the living room where he was tapping on a laptop.

"Ugh. I got stung. Going to my room," I said.

"You allergic?" he asked.

"Nope, but it's starting to hurt."

He walked over and examined my face, which was getting very hot.

"Oh, yeah. You're swelling already."

Great. Just what I needed. A bee sting right near my eye. This was going to be fun.

I headed down the hall, Ozzy right on my heels.

"Prop your head up on a pillow. That might help," Turk called after me.

"Yeah, okay."

I'd left my flowers on the kitchen counter.

I lay down while icing my cheek, wondering how much more shit the universe was going to throw at me. My skin was getting tighter and more uncomfortable around the swelling, and the ice was melting fast.

Before I went to get fresh ice, I took a look in my bathroom mirror. One side of my face was so swollen, my eye was nearly shut.

Lovely.

I stuck my head outside my bedroom door and heard the guys getting ready for dinner.

"Hey, Alessia, you joining us?" Remy asked.

"No thanks." I hustled into the kitchen, grabbed a bunch of ice, and started heading back to my room.

"Whoa!" Dash yelled. "Let me see that."

Fine.

I turned to face them all.

"Jesus."

"That looks painful."

"Damn."

I turned on my heel to head back to my room. Screw them if they thought I'd let them stare at me over dinner.

They already felt sorry enough for me.

I lay back on my bed and continued icing my face, which Ozzy kept trying to lick.

There was a tapping at my door.

"Alessia? It's Remy. I brought you some dinner."

Ohthankgod. I was starving. But not starving enough to overcome my vanity.

"Come in," I called.

He entered with a plate covered in a napkin and a small bowl for the dog.

"Wow, Remy, this is really nice. Thank you."

He held up a little plastic bottle and shook it back and forth. Little pink pills rattled around.

"How about some antihistamine? It may help with the reaction."

"Oh, yes, thank you."

Ozzy dove into her dinner, just like I did.

"Hey, would you like me to take you on a hike tomorrow? I'll try to keep you away from bees," he said.

"Oh, that would be great. Ozzy will enjoy it, too."

"Okay, then. Hope the pills help."

"Thanks, Remy. I really appreciate it."

Such nice thing to do, especially for a houseguest who wasn't even really supposed to be there.

I vowed to make more of an effort with myself as soon as my face was better. I'd learned a lot about hair and makeup on the stupid show. Might as well put my knowledge to work.

I opened the bag of items I'd picked up at the drugstore and pulled everything out. Pretty soon, my table was covered with everything a girl could want for hair and makeup.

Most useful thing I'd gotten out of *The Mating Game*.

CHAPTER 8

REMY

I'd have to thank Turk for taking Alessia shopping because in her new duds, it was like a butterfly had emerged from a cocoon of grey baggy sweats. Her short T-shirt revealed a tiny sliver of toned stomach, and her denim shorts hugged her ass like an upside down heart. Her long dark hair was pulled into a fat braid that she'd pulled over her shoulder, and her green eyes glittered in the high sun.

With her little backpack slung over one shoulder and Ozzy nipping at her heels, I was happy to let her take the lead on our hike. We guys came across few women on Savage Mountain, must less little hotties like the one I was following. I was going to enjoy my eye candy for as long as I could.

"Where does this trail go?" Alessia asked over her shoulder. She still had a red mark on her face from a bee sting, but to be honest, it was kind of cute.

"You'll see. There's a little surprise at the end."

"You sure you wouldn't rather lead? I mean, you know the way. I sure don't."

Was I busted? "I'd rather let you set the pace," I said.

I'd also rather watch her cute little butt jiggle, but I was keeping that thought to myself.

We continued on the trail without a sound except for the sweet-smelling pine needles flexing under our feet and the occasional whine or snort from Ozzy.

"Alessia, did you have dogs growing up?"

She laughed. "No. But I saw this one and I don't know—it was like I was obsessed. I had to have her."

"I thought Ozzy was Turk's dog."

She stopped on the trail and turned to face me. "Well, I think she's mine now," she said and continued walking.

Good save. Those two hadn't fooled anyone. Turk was about the last person in the world to bring home a dog.

"What about you?" she asked.

We continued walking. "Yeah, we had lots of dogs. I'm not sure what happened to them, though. They were all sent away somewhere."

"What do you mean?"

"I dropped out of college and joined the military. My parents were so pissed, they got rid of all the pets. There really wasn't anyone around anymore to take care of them, anyway. Except for the household staff."

Hopefully, Ozzy would fare better.

"Ugh. Can we rest a minute? This hill is killing me. And I thought I was in shape."

I had to say, I never knew perspiration could be so cute, and damn if Alessia wasn't a little honey with her face all shiny and a couple drops running down her temples. And I don't know what it was, but she smelled incredible. Clean girl with just a hint of soap and sweaty hard work.

"So, why were they mad, your parents?"

God, she was standing so close, it was all I could do to hide my giant goddamn erection.

I shrugged. "I didn't want to go into the family business. When they found out, they flipped and pretty much wrote me off. My brother Cap did the same thing. We were both cast out as the prodigal sons."

Shit. It was still painful to think back on that time. It had been as if you could belong to their club if you followed their plan for your life. Any deviation, and you get kicked off the island. So to speak.

While the family business had looked like the worst kind of drudgery from my twenty-year-old perspective, I sometimes think about how it would have been the path of least resistance—go to work for dad, inherit the company, marry someone from the club, churn out two-point-five children. And so on.

Bam.

Yeah, it would have been an easier life than quitting school and enlisting in the military, but I would have been beyond miserable. And so would everyone around me. So there was that.

When it all went down, I hadn't handled it in the most graceful way. Without saying anything to my parents, I just stopped going to classes mid-semester and got a job as a bouncer at the local strip club. I had no experience dealing with belligerent drunks, but I was a big guy, strong too, and the club was glad to have me. All I had to do was pretty much look at a trouble-maker and the dude would shape up. And when he didn't, he got booted out on his ass. By me.

When my parents got wind of my new life, it wasn't pretty. They flipped out, as if I'd joined a cult or was doing something illegal. They just had no ability to conceive of a life different from their own, and they sure didn't know why I'd consider one when they'd done so much to set me up for success. Success in their eyes, that was.

They cut me off from my allowance and told me not to come home. In my stubbornness and desire to show them I didn't need their largesse, I signed up with the military for the adventure but also to give my parents one last middle finger. My brother, who'd also been cut off, headed to Alaska to work on fishing boats.

Not the most mature way to handle things, but I had to make my own way.

Which was kind of a joke because I was, basically, a rich kid trying to act like a street-smart tough guy.

"So, you have no contact with them?" Alessia asked.

"Not really. I get the occasional birthday card from my mother. But they're getting older. I'd like to find a way to get back into their lives. I am in touch with my brother, Cap. I'm hoping he'll come visit this year."

We resumed walking.

"Wow. I would have thought they'd come around after some time," she said.

"I know. Me, too."

Eventually, the trail we were on opened into a big field.

"Wow. What is this?" she asked, scanning the horizon.

It was time for her to know a bit more about who we were and what we did.

"This is our firing range."

Her head snapped in my direction, and she furrowed her brow. "Um. Why do you need a firing range?"

I gestured toward a couple benches. "C'mon. Let's have a seat here."

She sat, pulling Ozzy up on her lap. The little

bugger kept jumping to mine and licking my face. She was so cute, it was impossible to get mad.

"We guys have a business that requires us to deal with some not very nice people. To do that, we need to be armed when we go on missions. We have this firing range to keep up our skills."

Her eyes widened. "Well, what exactly do you do?"

It was always a tricky balance, trying to figure out how much someone really wanted to know when they asked that question.

"We do work for the US military, other governments, and certain companies and individuals—work like protecting people in dangerous situations from unsavory people. Top-secret shit. Our missions get pretty intense. I'm afraid that's about all I can tell you."

"Oh. Right." She looked away nervously.

I normally wouldn't have shared info like that, but with Alessia living under our roof, she deserved to know why we were adamant about security and why we sometimes came off as mysterious or otherwise acted like assholes.

So, while I hadn't told her a whole lot, she now had enough info to fill in the blanks, herself.

I was eager to change the subject. "So, inquiring minds want to know. Did you really leave a guy at the altar?"

She chuckled. "Yeah, pretty much. He wasn't quite at the altar. He'd just entered the church, and I slipped out the side door and into the limo he'd just gotten out of and took off. I'd been given photos of him with another woman just minutes earlier."

"Jesus, that's awful."

She looked down at her hands and nodded. "Yeah, it's pretty fucked up. I got the limo to drive as far as they could take me. They dropped me at the bar where Dash found me. Since then, I've found out the whole show was staged. Reality shows are totally rigged. The guy wasn't into me at all. He had another woman. The producers put him up to it. Seems my 'girl next-door face' attracts viewers. People want to 'root' for me."

She wiped her face with the back of her hand, and I realized she was crying.

I draped an arm around her shoulders. "Sorry. I shouldn't have brought it up."

She rested her head on my shoulder for a moment, then looked up at me.

A moment later, her lips were on mine.

Holy shit.

That, I was not expecting.

After a moment, she pulled away, giving me the chance to look at her closer than I ever had.

"You're very beautiful, you know," I said.

She shook her head modestly. "No. I'm not. But thank you, Remy."

Was she fucking kidding? With her long dark hair and bright eyes, she was a goddamn knockout. And I wasn't saying that just because I hadn't seen a pretty girl in awhile.

Or kissed one, for that matter.

So, I returned my lips to hers and damn if she wasn't just as delicious as I thought she'd be, her mouth soft and pliant under mine, her tongue responding eagerly when I explored with my own.

I wove my fingers into her hair, and my now-raging erection was fucking killing me. I smoothed my hands down her back to cup her ass while Ozzy jumped down to chase a butterfly.

And that was it.

I was a patient man and knew I needed to take my time with this lovely woman.

"Hey, Alessia, want to chop some more onions for me?" I threw several cans of tomatoes into a giant pot in preparation for my famous spaghetti sauce.

"Yeah," she said, topping off both our glasses of red wine.

It was nice to see her enjoying the top-notch zinfandel I'd opened. However, she looked like she might be enjoying it a bit too much.

She waved an onion around in one hand and a large knife in another. Note to self: keep an eye on this one before she hurts herself or someone else.

"You know, Remy, all you guys are hot as hell. I mean, seriously. How do you not have women pounding your doors down?"

Ah. She was one of those. Alcohol loosens lips, big time.

But *I* couldn't really say anything. God knew I'd been in the same shape once or twice in my life.

"Well, thank you, Alessia. But please, be careful with that knife."

She put it down, and I took the opportunity to slide it over to my side of the counter, out of her reach.

Leaning closer, hair spilling around her shoulders, she lowered her voice to a whisper. She looked around the room, as if it were full of people who might hear her.

"Do you guys… you know, play for the other team? If you do, I'm totally cool with that." She held her hands up like a *stop* sign. "Sorry I kissed you today. I should have known when you pulled back that you weren't into girls."

Her face asked for forgiveness as she took another gulp of her wine.

"Alessia, I'm not gay. Nor are the other guys."

She rolled her eyes. "Remy, seriously, I'm cool with it. I love gay guys."

I set up a small pan to cook the onions. "If I were, I'd tell you, Alessia. It's not the kind of thing I'd ever keep from people."

She squinted at me. "Really? Are you sure?"

Oh, for Christ's sake.

At the smell of tomatoes and onions cooking, it was no surprise that the other guys in the house soon found their way to the kitchen, with Ozzy running from one to the other, hoping for some sort of treat. Alessia cheerfully outfitted everyone with his own glass of wine, and I popped open another bottle.

"Cheers," Alessia slurred, holding her glass up. "You guys rock. And whether you're gay or not, I don't care. You're fucking hot, and I love you all."

Amused expressions crossed the guys' faces, and they looked at me with raised eyebrows.

I shrugged. "I tried to tell her—"

"Fucking A, I tried to kiss him when we were on a walk, and he looked like he was going to throw up—"

All right. The evening was over for a certain beautiful brunette who couldn't hold her wine.

"Alessia, that's not true. Now, come on. It's time for you to go to bed. Dash, will you stir the sauce for me until I get back?

I walked Alessia to her room, my arm around her shoulders, and hers awkwardly encircling my waist. Ozzy trotted faithfully behind us.

"You guys are so great. I really do love you."

"Thank you," I said. "Here. Let me get your shoes off," I said, when we'd gotten to her room.

"Remy?" she asked, looking up at me while I tucked her in.

"Yeah?"

"You're really not gay?"

I shook my head.

"Can I have a kiss goodnight, then?"

I bent to kiss her for the second time that day, but this time, I was determined to let her know how much I wanted her. Our lips touched, and as soon as I found hers pliable and willing, I pressed into her with a fury that left no doubt about my interest.

CHAPTER 9

ALESSIA

I made my way to breakfast the next morning, walking slowly and carefully so as not to shake my throbbing, hungover brain.

But I stopped short of the kitchen when I heard my name mentioned. I wasn't normally one to eavesdrop, but the tone I heard made me realize I'd better tread lightly. Or, actually just leave Savage Mountain.

"It's just too big of a security risk having her here," Forrest said.

Why was that guy always on my ass?

"Well, I had a talk with her when we were out walking. I showed her the firing range and explained about our business," Remy said.

What a guy, defending me. Now I was super-glad I'd kissed him.

"When I took her to town the other day, I stressed how important security was to us. She seemed to understand it pretty clearly, especially when some guy from the reality show was hounding her to reveal her location," Turk added.

"Dash, what do you think?" Forrest asked.

C'mon Dash!

He took a deep breath. "I'm kind of on the fence. She *is* a security risk. There's no doubt about it. But if it's a managed risk, that's much easier to stomach. If we're vigilant and make sure she understands what's at stake, then there shouldn't be any problems."

Fuck yeah. I'd won them all over. Well, with the exception of Forrest. But three out of four was pretty damn good. I wasn't going to complain.

But I *was* going to make some changes.

Dash continued. "I'd hate to see her leave. She's drop-dead gorgeous and nice to hang out with. And it sounds like she got the message from Turk, that she needs to be discreet and not let anyone follow her up here."

Just then, Ozzy came running up to me, giving away my hiding place.

"Good morning, all," I said cheerfully, bounding into the room like I'd just arrived.

They wouldn't know I was eavesdropping, would they?

"Good morning, Alessia," Remy said. "Hey, we were just talking about your stay here."

"Oh, really?" I raised my eyebrows in fake surprise.

"I was just thinking about it, too," I continued. "Not sure how long I'll be here because I don't know when the media will let up. So for as long as I'm here, I want to earn my keep."

The guys looked at each other, not having anticipated my offer.

Turk smiled. "How do you propose to do that, Alessia?"

Think fast.

I looked around the house. "Seems like you guys could use some help with a little cleaning…"

I had to be careful about what I signed up for. I hated cleaning. Wasn't very good at it, either.

They looked at each other. Dash nodded, and Forrest shrugged.

I had to admit, I also had a few dirty thoughts in mind since I now knew the guys—well, at least, Remy—liked girls. I mean, why not? They were fucking hot, and I might as well have some fun while I was sequestered in the mountains. After I left, I'd never see them again, anyway.

I'd be crazy to pass up gorgeous men like these ones, especially since I'd nearly married someone who didn't give a shit about me. And to be honest, Montgomery wasn't that great in bed, with his tiny dick and rabbit humping moves.

I was ready for a real man. Or real *men,* to be more accurate.

"Lady, hey, it's me," I said from my special cell phone-friendly spot.

"Alessia, hi. I'm at work. Let me go somewhere I can talk," she whispered.

The usual sounds of the car rental agency came through the phone, and I realized I missed the place, even though it wasn't the best job in the world. I longed for something familiar and safe, and it dawned on me how long I'd been away from everything I knew, with both my time on the show and now at the cabin.

A lump grew in my throat. "I miss you, Lady. I miss everything about home, actually."

"I miss you too, girlfriend, but I'd stay away if I were you. There are still cameras out front, looking for you. It's crazy. You'd think they'd get tired of it after a while."

When was it going to stop?

I sat down on a log, and Ozzy made herself at home on my feet. "So, I talked to the guys about hanging out here a bit longer. I offered to help around the house. Clean a bit. You know, stuff like that."

"But you hate housework. Your own apartment is a pigsty."

"Thanks, Lady. That's really nice," I said.

She laughed. "Well, you know what I mean. You clean like once a year."

"Whatever. Anyway, I was thinking, if I was gonna be up here for longer, I might see if I can initiate a little hanky panky. You know, with the guys."

She gasped. "Oh, my god. Brilliant. Get Mont off your mind."

"Oh, I've already forgotten about that pencil dick."

"That's my girl. Hey, what are the chances I could come visit you? You know, get a taste of life in the mountains for myself?" she asked.

Yeah, she was curious about the mountains, my ass.

"Lady, I told you they're not big on visitors here."

"Oh, c'mon. Try," she pleaded. "Anyway, now you have to get to a store and buy some sexy stuff. Show off your cute little moneymaker, girl. Torture those mountain men and show them what they've been missing. Make 'em feel good. They are hosting you, after all. A little nookie might be good for you with all you've just come through."

Maybe Lady was right. A little mountain fun could be just what the doctor ordered.

And then, maybe, I wouldn't have to clean, after all.

CHAPTER 10

DASH

"So, are ya pretty much settled into the house? All good?" I asked Alessia as I steered us down the mountain to run some errands.

She flashed me her pretty smile from the passenger seat of my truck. Damn, she was gorgeous, and with the way she was sitting, her little skirt was, um, rather short.

Down boy.

"Things are great, Dash, and the cabin is amazing. I'm very grateful for all you and the guys have done. I don't know what would have happened if you hadn't stuck up for me back in that bar. Those men were scary and the waitress and bartender couldn't have cared less. Ugh. What a day that was."

She leaned down and kissed her puppy. "Ozzy is grateful, too."

"Well, I'm enjoying having you at our place. Glad it's working out. I knew it would. I'm sure you figured out we don't usually have guests, but in this case, I knew I could convince the guys it was okay."

I'd known from the start she'd be a fine addition to the house—nothing long-term of course—but a little female energy would do us all some good. That is, except for Forrest, who was generally pretty happy steeping in his misery.

I pulled into town and parked in front of the general store. "This where you wanted to go?"

She laughed. "Well, there aren't exactly a lot of choices here. But yes, this is fine."

She turned to me in her seat before getting out. "Hey, how'd you end up in the cabin? You former military like the other guys?"

I put the car in *park* and got comfortable. "Well, I was kind of a computer nerd, and founded a security start-up when I was still in college."

Her eyes popped open, and she laughed. "No way. In a garage? And then you dropped out of school, right? To make the big bucks?"

She had my number.

"Pretty much. Typical computer nerd story. My buddies and I developed a threat analysis protocol that ended up getting a lot of attention, much to our surprise. I mean, when we developed it, it was more of a whim than anything. We weren't sure anyone would ever use it—"

Her rapt attention was driving me crazy. She was truly interested in what I was talking about, which I did not expect. Not at all.

"So," I continued, "a private security firm started by a bunch of ex-military special ops guys needed a hacker like me. Someone who could run digital intel for them, keep their clients' systems safe. They picked me, bought out my technology, and I've been with Forrest, Turk, and Remy ever since."

"You're a *hacker*?" she asked with wide eyes.

I had to laugh at that. "Yeah, I am, but it's probably not what you think."

She tilted her head. "Really?"

"Well, a lot of people think hacker equals criminal. But it's not that simple. Hacker really means you basically solve computer problems. There are good people who do that and some bad. Governments, companies, and individuals hire people like me to make sure their systems are secure. Basically, I get paid to try to break in, so that clients know where their weaknesses, threats, and vulnerabilities are."

"But what about hackers who steal personal information and money?"

"There are plenty of those out there, too. But they are the ones hackers like me are fighting against. I consider myself an ethical hacker. I'm not manipulating systems for my own gain. I'm not stealing any information to make money off of. My work helps keep people safe from harm."

"I get it. That is so cool. We once had someone hack into our rental system at work. It was a mess. But I guess, essentially, the person who cleaned it all up was something of a hacker himself."

Smart girl.

"Exactly. He'd have to understand how someone broke in in order to shore up that weakness and prevent it from happening again."

She opened the car door and began to step out. "Okay. I want to learn more about this. It's fascinating. But let me run into this store here. You coming with, or waiting?"

"Nah. I think I'll take a walk around the block with Ozzy. I'll meet you back here in fifteen."

"Okay," she said with a wink and skipped off to the mercantile.

Christ, if I'd had more privacy, I might have rubbed one out, that's how turned on she had me.

I watched her disappear into the store and strike up a conversation with the clerk inside. They smiled at each other and disappeared into the racks of clothing where I could no longer see them.

There was something about Alessia. She'd been through a lot, but she was stoic about the choices she'd made and was bravely charging through the fallout. I had to give her props for that.

Personally, I couldn't imagine having my personal life on display for the world to see, but then, when Alessia entered that arena, she probably didn't know how things were going to play out, either.

After twenty minutes or so, I poked my head into the store.

The clerk who was helping Alessia called to me. "Hello sir, come on in. We're just finishing up."

"Hey, Dash," Alessia called from the dressing room.

I waved at her and was looking around for a place to sit when the clerk sidled up to me. "Your wife is making some great selections, sir."

"What? Oh, she's not my wife."

Her eyes widened, and she looked me up and down. "Oh. Well, you'll be glad to know your friend is a very good shopper."

That was one diplomatic clerk.

"Glad to hear it."

She hustled off to the dressing room, leaving me standing amidst a bunch of ladies' underwear.

But she wasn't as discrete as she thought she was.

And I was a natural eavesdropper.

"Miss, your friend out there is very handsome," she said once she was back in the room with Alessia.

"Oh, yeah, he is. Hey, do you think I could see this in pink?" she asked

I didn't know what they were doing in there, but I

was having a great time imagining.

"You know, miss," the clerk continued, "you're a beautiful woman. You could make this lingerie work for you. You know, on the gentleman waiting for you?"

Holy crap. The clerk was coaching Alessia. This was awesome shit. I moved a couple steps closer.

"You do? I mean, he's really great. I was kind of hoping all these pretty things might make the guys—I mean Dash out there—sit up and take notice of me."

"Oh, I have no doubt he'll notice you, if he hasn't already."

Alessia laughed. "Here's hoping."

I had to bite my tongue to keep from laughing. Our girl had a little plan up her sleeve. Perhaps she'd be enjoying our cozy hideaway more than everyone originally thought.

And had I heard her correctly that she wanted *all* of us to take notice of her?

Now *that* was fucking hot.

On the way back up the mountain, she seemed very interested in my hacking work.

"Dash, is it hard to learn this stuff?" she asked.

Was the woman looking for a new profession? Renting cars would not cut it after weeks as a TV star?

"Well, you have to have an interest in computer science. And I'd say you have to be pretty good at it, too. You know, have a passion for solving puzzles. When your first approach doesn't work, you need to be driven to try another, and another. That doesn't work for some people. Others, like me, thrive on figuring shit out. When I was younger, I'd sometimes skip sleep for days, that's how obsessed I got with cracking a challenge wide open."

She nodded slowly.

"Why do you ask? You looking for a new profession?" I asked, half jokingly.

"No. No, I'm not. Just thinking it sounded really cool and much more challenging than the work I do."

I reached over and patted her leg. "Oh, I don't know. I am sure you have some good stories to tell about your work. And that you get to drive some pretty sweet cars."

A smile spread across her face. "Well, yeah, when no one's around, we try the cars out in the parking lot and stuff. But to be honest, that novelty wears off pretty soon. After a while, you just don't care. It's like you look at cars differently. They're no longer toys or status symbols. They are just means for getting around, and expensive money-sucking ones, at that."

"You have a point," I said.

Fuck, I wanted to pull over and kiss her.

But I'd wait. I was not particularly patient, but I knew to bide my time. Maybe she'd show me the lingerie she'd bought, since the clerk had hinted around at seduction.

Maybe she'd show *all* of us. I'd seen her checking the guys and me out once or twice. If she was trying to be sneaky about it, she needed to try a little harder.

"Dash, could you—"

She stopped.

"What? Could I what?" I asked.

She took a deep breath before she spoke. "Could you do something with your hacking skills to my ex? The guy who was supposed to marry me?"

Later that night, for the first time since she'd been with us, Alessia sat down to watch TV with us.

And don't you know, Forrest turned on *The Mating Game*.

Fucking idiot.

The rest of us guys—Turk, Remy, and me—looked at each other and then nervously at Alessia.

"Um, are you sure you want to watch this?" I asked.

"Oh, it's probably just a re-run," she said with a little too much confidence.

Her assumption was quickly proven wrong. The producer, Billy, sat down for an interview with Mont, in a studio-like setting, surrounded by several beautiful women.

"Who are they?" Turk asked.

Alessia's face was pale, and she looked like she might be sick. "The women? Um, they were contestants on the show with me. The blonde is Vanessa, who was supposed to be in my wedding."

I didn't have a good feeling about this.

"Guys, maybe we should turn this off—"

"No," she interrupted. "I want to see it."

I think it was more the case that she felt she *needed* to see the show, rather than *wanted* to. Regardless, I had the feeling she was setting herself up for something unpleasant.

"So, Mont," the blustery producer said, "it looks like you're in the doghouse." He smiled at the camera and shuffled some large index cards in his hands.

Mont, a wiry guy with preppy, slicked-back hair, laughed and slapped his knee. "Dude. I'm so far beyond being in the doghouse. I mean, I'm in such deep trouble, there isn't a doghouse big enough for me and my trouble."

Billy tilted his head with fake concern. "Are you upset, Mont? That Alessia took off on you? I mean, it can't feel good."

But Mont just laughed. "Well, you know, it was probably for the better that I let her off the hook. It just wouldn't have worked."

"What? He *let me off the hook*?" Alessia screamed, jumping out of her seat. "I left that fucker at the church. Everybody knows that."

Billy leaned forward as if they were sharing a secret. "Yeah, I can see what you mean. She really loved you. You could just see it in her eyes." He shook his head sadly.

"Look," Mont said, "I feel for her. I don't think any of us meant to hurt her."

I glanced at Alessia, whose mouth was wide open.

Billy turned to the women. "What do you ladies think?"

One, in a low cut top, sporting giant breast implants, chimed in. "Guys. Did you really think it would work with her? I mean she just fell off a turnip truck, for heaven's sake."

Billy and Mont looked at each other, and then fell back in their chairs, cracking up.

Holy shit.

"She never would have appreciated you," she said to Mont, batting her eyes.

Not wanting to be forgotten, Vanessa chimed in. "Look, guys. She was an idiot. There were other women on the show who were a much better match for Mont. Everyone knew it. Everyone but Alessia," she said, rolling her eyes and shaking her head.

"Holy fucking shit," Alessia murmured, her gaze glued to the TV.

And Forrest decided it was time to make things worse.

"Aw, c'mon Alessia, what did you think was going to happen? I mean, what did you expect from putting yourself out there like that?"

Uh-oh.

Alessia walked up to where Forrest was sitting and got right in his face.

Game on.

"What did you just say to me?" she growled.

His eyes widened, and he sat back in his chair.

"Well, c'mon, Alessia. These shows are ridiculous." His eyes darted around from one of us to the other, as if he were looking for support.

He wasn't going to get any from me. I was hoping the fucker would learn to think before he opened his big mouth next time.

Alessia leaned closer to him. "You think I don't regret participating in that *garbage*?" She gestured the TV, which Turk had turned off. "Forrest, you think I don't wake up every morning trying to figure a way out of the goddamn nightmare my life has become? Because I do. Those weren't nice people I got involved with, and you're not a nice person either, sitting there enjoying my pain like the smug fuck that you are."

Forrest was silent.

"So go *fuck yourself*!" she screamed so loudly his head snapped back.

Tears streamed down her face, and her fists clenched so hard, her fingers were white. Time to intervene.

I put my hand on Alessia's arm. "C'mon. Let me take you to your room." I led her out of the living room, and she followed me without resistance with Ozzy right behind, not sure what to make of the screaming.

"And Forrest?" I called over my shoulder.

He looked up at me.

"She's right. You are a fucking asshole."

CHAPTER 11

ALESSIA

"I'm sorry, Dash," I sniffled.

I took another tissue from him. "I lost my shit. I should not have yelled at Forrest. And I shouldn't be crying on your shoulder. You were so nice to take me shopping today. You don't deserve to get wrapped up in my drama. You should have just left me at that bar in my wedding dress."

I lay back on my bed and looked up at my room's ornate ceiling. I wanted him to leave because I was a huge fucking idiot, but I also wanted him to stay.

I looked at him, perched on the edge of my bed. "So what is wrong with Forrest, anyway? He has a jerk streak about a mile long."

To my surprise, Dash plopped down on the bed next to me, turning on his side to face me. "He can be a real asshole, you are right. You know, he lost his dad on 9/11."

"Oh. Shit."

"Yeah," Dash said, nodding. "He never got over it. He joined the military when he was old enough, got into special ops, and then moved into private security when his tour was up. He saw some seriously ugly shit. He lost a part of himself. It happens to some warriors."

I wandered my fingers across the bed and touched his. "Awful. What about you? Did you have to do the things he did?"

He shook his head. "I was in a computer lab most of the time geeking out behind the scenes. Never been on the front lines. Thank god. My job paid really well but I'll tell you, sometimes I feel like I worked for blood money."

I was trying to listen to what Dash was telling me but his dark eyes and perfectly sculpted chin were such a freaking distraction. And he smelled so good. Nothing fancy. Just plain soap and yummy guy.

And then, don't you know, he leaned closer. My heart slammed against my chest as his gaze drilled into me, and just before our lips met, a slight smile spread across his face.

His lips were soft on mine at first, and then became downright forceful. His hand wandered up my thigh and to my hip, where he grasped my waist in his giant palm.

"Mmmm," he murmured. "You're so beautiful, Alessia. You know how many times I've thought about kissing you?"

Oh, my god.

This gorgeous, smart, and kind man had thought about kissing *me*? And he was in my *bed*?

Just as I was marveling over my good fortune, he clasped my hands and pulled them up, over my head. He wedged himself between my legs, and through our clothes, his huge erection pressed against me.

I was pinned. And I liked it.

I wanted to see what this man would do to me, and to be honest, I was hoping it was something rough and dirty. I just wanted to forget all the shit that had been going down in my life, and this was one amazing way to feel better.

Plus, Dash was one gorgeous man. His arms flexed as he held me prisoner, and his eyes opened, then closed, as I pushed up against his constrained cock.

"You feel so good, baby," he murmured. "I want more."

I shimmied under him and smiled. "You do? Really? What more do you want?" I teased.

He lifted my T-shirt with his teeth and, thank god, I'd put on some of the sexy lingerie I'd bought earlier. In fact, I'd bought out all the store had, leaving the next shopper not much to choose from except white cotton granny panties that came three to a pack.

And my pretty bra had turned out to be a good investment, too. Dash sucked in a deep breath when he got a load of the black lace just covering my hard nipples. He inched one side down with his teeth and took me into his mouth.

A wave of sensation washed over me, leaving a throbbing between my legs that was going to have to be addressed before this man left my bedroom.

And as if he read my mind, he released my arms and pushed my little skirt up to my waist, revealing my new lace thong.

"Fucking A," he breathed and pushed the delicate fabric aside, exposing my wet pussy.

Without hesitation, he buried his tongue in my slick folds.

"Oh, Dash, oh my god," I mumbled. "That feels so good."

I pushed my hips into his face for more, and he reciprocated by zeroing in on my clit, licking and sucking until I screamed.

"God, Dash, yes, I'm coming," I hollered, my fists pounding the bed under me, my upset of earlier in the evening long forgotten.

He sat up long enough to pull the rest of my clothes off, and smiled. "Well, look at you, gorgeous. Baby's got no clothes." He leaned down to kiss me again.

Damn if this guy wasn't the sexiest man I'd ever

been with. His confidence and power made me shake with need, something not lost on him as he lifted his shirt over his own head, tossing it to the floor on my pile of clothes. I leaned up on my elbows as he opened his fly and pushed his jeans down, revealing an erection that bounced against his tummy.

"What are you gonna do with that huge thing?" I teased.

Seriously.

"Well," he said, balancing over me. "I could do nothing with it. But that would seem like such a waste."

I nodded in agreement.

"Or, I could put a condom on and fuck the shit out of you."

Had I not been lying down, I would certainly have fallen over at that moment.

I reached down between us and grasped his hard cock, sliding my fingers up and down it with a light, teasing touch, hoping my torment would drive him wild.

"If you don't put this to good use, that could be very bad for us both," I whispered.

He pushed his cock in and out of my soft grip, and I knew I had to have him inside me.

He reached for his jeans, pulled a condom out of his pocket, and rolled it on. He notched himself at my opening but stopped. "You wanna guide me in, beautiful girl?"

Well, that's all he had to say because if he hadn't fucked me right then, I would have lost my damn mind.

I held him as he entered me an inch.

Not the time to take things slow.

"Fuck me, Dash," I whispered.

With a thrust of his hips, he buried himself in me up to his balls.

I convulsed as pleasure gushed through my belly and radiated to every pore, my breath coming in deep gasps. I slammed my head against the bed as another orgasm overtook me.

Dash pounded me with his cock, my juices flowing over us both. I put my hands on either side of his face, and he pressed his lips to mine as I came again.

"God, your pussy's tight, baby. I'm gonna come. Fuck," he growled, pistoning me so hard I had to hold on with all my strength.

We collapsed, and after a moment, he pulled back the bed covers for me and climbed in right behind.

I'd heard Dash leave my room early in the morning when he'd bent over me with a sweet kiss, pulled the comforter up to my chin, and quietly slipped out after scratching behind Ozzy's ears.

I could have slept longer—probably a lot longer—but Ozzy needed to go out.

"C'mon, girl," I said, yawning, as I pulled on clothes.

"Good morning," I called as I wandered through the house.

No one was around.

It wasn't unusual in the few days I'd been there for the house to be pretty quiet in the morning. But it was the first time I'd gotten up and no one was around.

I followed Ozzy up the path I'd walked on with Remy the day before and munched on the English muffin I'd grabbed from the kitchen. Just when I heard a rustling, I whipped around to check on her. I spotted a deer take off through the woods, with my fierce little puppy barking right on its tail.

"Ozzy! Come back here!" I said, running after her.

Luckily, she was too small to move very fast, and while the deer was long gone, she wasn't giving up easily. When I finally caught her, we were outside a building I'd never noticed before on the property.

It was an ugly, utilitarian structure, made of simple cinderblocks. I inched up to it and through the open window saw the guys on a video call.

Was this related to whatever weird, secret business they were in?

"We always promise our informants rides across the border, Jack. That's non-negotiable. I'm sorry," Dash said sternly, to someone on screen.

A male voice on the other end of the line responded, but I couldn't make out what he was saying.

"The funds must be deposited in an off-shore trust.

We'll get you the account information," Forrest said. "Other than that, I think we're all set—"

Just then, Ozzy spotted the deer, and went crazy barking.

"Shhh, Ozzy!" I hissed.

But it was too late. The conversation in the cinderblock building came to an abrupt halt.

"Jack, we'll pick this back up later," Forrest said.

Shit.

I scooped Ozzy up in my arms and started race-walking back to the house.

"Hold it!" Forrest called.

Damn.

All four guys walked toward me, and while I figured I was in trouble, I couldn't deny that my heart beat a little faster knowing their eyes were on me. And they looked stern. So very stern.

Even Dash, whom I'd just spent the night with.

"Hey, guys!" I said brightly.

Might as well at least *act* innocent.

"Just taking Ozzy out for a little pee break. How are you guys this morning?" I chirped.

"Alessia, you're not supposed to be in this area. Were you listening in on our meeting?" Remy asked.

"No," I said, shaking my head. "Nope. Ozzy took off after a deer, and I followed her here. We were just heading back to the house."

Forrest's hand closed on my arm. "Okay. Let's go," he said.

I tried to wrench myself out of his grip. "Hey, get off me. I can get back to the house without your help."

But he didn't let go.

So, I turned at looked at the other guys, appealing with my eyes.

But they looked equally as displeased.

"Guys. I'm not sure what I did wrong, but it wasn't intentional."

Forrest's grip did not lessen, and the expressions the guys wore remained just as stern.

Fuck all. Maybe I should have just married Mont. I'd be stuck with a cheating bastard of a husband, but at least I'd be safe from a bunch of mercenary psychos, and I'd have gotten all the money I earned from that fucking show.

Instead, just when I thought things couldn't get any worse, they did.

CHAPTER 12

FORREST

A lessia tried, unsuccessfully, to hip-chuck me. "You can stop manhandling me, now. No one's looking, okay?"

I jerked her by the arm, probably harder than I had to. But I was beyond pissed. "You need to respect our lives here on the mountain. We do top-secret work, which means you need to be careful where you tread."

"Why are you such a jerk, Forrest? Everyone else here is nice enough and then there's you."

I ignored her goading. If there was one thing I'd learned from the Special Forces, it was not to fall prey to someone trying to provoke me.

"C'mon," I said, guiding her into the cabin. "I'm taking you to your room."

"Fine. Take me to my room. But don't think for one second you are welcome inside. If you step one foot over the threshold, I'll scream for help."

Christ. Entering her room was about the last damn thing on my mind. I wanted this woman out of my face… and out of our lives.

When we reached her door, I looked right at her. "Listen, Alessia. I know you've been through a lot. And you seem like a nice person. But you need to take responsibility for your actions. This isn't some sort of amusement park. There are serious things at play that you have no visibility into. Things you don't know about, and believe me, don't *want* to know about."

"Fine. Whatever, Forrest. If you think I'm that interested in your little world here, you have another thought coming. I could care less about you, and whatever mysterious work you do. I'm having someone come get me. I can't take this place and all your secrets any longer," she said.

I took a deep breath to check my dwindling patience. "That, Alessia, is where you're wrong. Not only are you not inviting anyone up here, you are also not leaving."

I got her to her room, with Ozzy on her heels.

"You can't make me stay here," she said defiantly.

"Actually, we can. Until we decide what to do with you, since you so freely eavesdropped on a sensitive and top-secret meeting, you will be closed in your room here. If you need anything, knock and we'll do our best to accommodate you. But we can't risk having you stumble upon any more of our activities. It's dangerous for us and dangerous for you."

She looked over my shoulder at the guys standing behind me, desperate. "C'mon guys. Help me out," she pleaded.

I turned to see them shaking their heads.

"Can't Alessia. Sorry," Remy said.

Her face turned bright red with anger. "Don't you all know I could give a shit about your little fantasy world up here? I don't know anything about it, nor do I care to," she shouted.

Ozzy must have been upset by the yelling, because she lunged at my leg.

"Oh, Ozzy!" Alessia exclaimed, running to scoop her up. "See, you even have her upset now. Just go. Leave us alone," she said, waving us away.

"If you need anything, knock. But we are locking you in your room, Alessia."

With that, I pulled her door shut and turned the key.

As we guys made our way back to the kitchen, Turk turned to me. "Forrest, do you think this is taking the discipline thing too far?"

"I don't think so, Turk. Hopefully, she'll be gone soon, but until then, we need to keep her out of our business. One misstep and she could take down all we've worked so hard for. I mean, seriously, Turk. Do you remember the days when you weren't even making enough money to replace your old, broken-down truck? And yet, you'd been shot for your country? We get high-paying missions now, and I know *I'm* not willing to lose that."

While we guys were finally in agreement on keeping Alessia in her room, at least for the time being, starving her was not part of the plan. As soon as that night's dinner came off the stove, I piled a plate high and brought it to her.

"Alessia?" I said, knocking lightly. "It's me, Forrest."

Well, *shit*. There was no mistaking the sounds coming from her room.

She was crying.

I was half–tempted to leave her plate at the door, but hell, she deserved better than that. "I, um, have some dinner for you, Alessia. Can I come in to give it to you?"

She sniffled loudly. "Yeah. Okay. Will you take Ozzy out? I think she has to go to the bathroom.

"Yeah, sure," I said, unlocking the door.

She pulled it open and, without looking at me, took the plate from my hand. Then she handed me Ozzy's leash.

"Thank you," she said and closed the door.

Ozzy looked up at me and whined. I wondered if she remembered earlier in the day, when she'd tried to bite me.

"Hey, you gonna eat?" Turk asked as I passed through the dining room to go outside with the dog.

"Yes, please. Could you make me a plate and just put some foil over it?"

"Yuppers. We got some good grub tonight," he said.

Remy laughed. "Yeah, that's because I cooked, you douchebag."

"Hey, I wasn't taking credit for your first *ever* culinary success—"

I left Turk and Remy arguing over who was the better cook and slipped outside with Ozzy. I wasn't thrilled having a dog in the house, but I had to admit she was a sweet little puppy and was catching on to her training.

I knew my dinner was probably beyond cold, but I found myself keeping Ozzy outside longer than she really needed. I surprised myself by wanting to avoid going back and facing Alessia. There was no doubt in my mind I'd either been the one to make her cry, or had at least contributed. I wanted to apologize for coming down hard like I did, but that was exactly the sort of thing I sucked at.

Man up, dickhead.

I headed back in and discovered all evidence of dinner cleaned up and put away. The only thing on the counter was my sad little dinner plate. I popped it into the fridge and made my way down the hall.

Not hearing anything from the other side of the

door, I knocked quietly. "Alessia? It's Forrest. I'm back with the dog."

"You can come in," she said.

I unlocked her door, and the dog barged in.

"Thanks for walking Ozzy," she said, turning back to her book.

"Um, Alessia, can we talk for a minute?" I asked.

She shrugged. "I guess so."

I took a seat in the easy chair next to her. "I wanted to say I'm sorry for coming down so hard on you."

She shrugged. "Okay. Thank you."

"I know I can be tough. Too tough, actually. I let my past get the better of me sometimes and forget to behave like a normal human."

She played with the dog, teasing her with a rolled-up sock.

I continued, wondering if she was listening. "I hope you can understand why we have such strict security measures here. Or, if you can't understand, at least accept that we have to do things a certain way. We have enemies because of the work we do, so have to take certain precautions. It's a matter of life and death for us, as well as for the people we work for. And as long as you're with us, you need to be careful, too."

She looked up, finally. "Why? Why me?"

"Because you know enough about us now, and our work, that you could be a target of our enemies, as well."

"Are you fucking kidding me?" she asked, frowning.

I shook my head. "I wish I were."

She looked down at her hands. "Man, I have to get the hell out of here."

I reached and put a hand on her arm. "I'm sorry, Alessia. Sorry you had to get involved in our world. That's why I protested your staying here. Not because I didn't like you or didn't want to help you. I knew what this could mean for you. On top of what you already have going on, I know this isn't fun to hear." I grasped her hands in mine. "I like having you here. I know it might not seem like it, but I do. You add a lot to the house. And you're drop dead gorgeous, besides."

Fuck. Why did I say that last bit?

My powers of seduction had never been as smooth as I'd like. Sure, I'd had plenty of women, but the ones I was really interested in seeing a second time were few and far between.

Having Alessia in the house and living with her for several days had done something to me.

I liked her.

And I was hoping she didn't completely hate me. But there was only one way to find out.

I hooked a finger under her chin and lifted her face toward mine.

"Will you let me keep you safe? If anything happened to you, I couldn't forgive myself."

Surprise washed over her face. "Y… yes. Of course. And I'll try not to make your life any harder than it already is."

"Okay, then. We've got a deal."

Now that I had her looking at me, I wasn't about to let her go. I wanted her… and badly.

So I leaned over to kiss her. Nothing dramatic, just a quick one, and then pulled back.

To my delight, her eyes were closed.

So I went for it.

I pressed my lips to hers again. She was soft and delicious, and all I could think of was wanting more. I slowly lay her back on the bed and hovered over her, kissing her with growing urgency.

"You're so beautiful," I whispered.

She reached up and ran her fingers through my hair. "I was just thinking the same about you."

CHAPTER 13

ALESSIA

Holy shit. Second night in a row making out with one of the guys. What were they going to think?

Actually, I didn't care. I'd be out of there soon enough, and they'd forget I ever intruded on their little paradise.

But in the meantime, there was plenty of fun to be had, and at that moment, no one was more excited than Forrest, whose giant hard-on ground against my thigh as he balanced over me, kissing my lips and neck.

And damn if his kisses weren't working their way down to the buttons of my blouse. Something about this gorgeous ogre of a man turned me on to no end. I mean, he always seemed so stern and in control, and to think he could soften when the occasion called for it and even make himself a bit vulnerable was damn irresistible.

Once he'd undone enough buttons to get to my bare breasts, he leaned back. A slight smile crossed his face as he looked me up and down with melting admiration. I don't think I'd ever felt so desirable, and to think, just a few hours before, he was so pissed at me he could barely string a sentence together.

I ran my fingers through his dark blond hair while he brushed my erect nipples with his mouth. His dimples belied the badass neck tattoo he wore and I couldn't decide if he looked more like a preppy frat boy or a hard-core rocker.

Or a combination of both.

I was never so happy as when he inched south toward my overheated core. I was dying for attention down there, and being impatient, opened my jeans and shimmied them down my hips.

"Damn. Baby's in a hurry." He pitched in by pulling my jeans the rest of the way off and dropping them to the floor.

Again, his eyes raked over me with appreciation and ended on my bare pussy, soaked with excitement.

"Now *your* clothes, if ya don't mind," I said.

He smiled devilishly, pulling his shirt over his head, revealing a rock-hard chest and giant biceps.

Jesus.

Next, he hopped off the bed while he undid he jeans. They fell to the floor in a pile, and damn if he hadn't been going commando. I could barely take my eyes off the beautiful cock bouncing against his thigh, complete with a drop of shiny precum at the tip.

He shoved my legs open and dove between them, burying his face in my juicy core. Shivers wracked my body from his licking and sucking, and when he pulled back, he leaned over me for a kiss so I could taste myself.

"You like it, baby?" he murmured.

All I could do was nod.

"Flip over," he growled.

On my hands and knees, I looked back over my shoulder to see him rolling on a condom he must have gotten out of his pants pocket.

"Down," he growled, pushing my head to the bed and picking my hips up so high that I was fully exposed.

"You good, baby?" he asked, running his fingers through my slick pussy lips.

I nodded. "I want more," I said, pushing against him.

"Yeah," he growled, notching himself at my opening

As he entered me, his fingers reached for my hard clit. As he massaged it, he steadily worked his way inside me.

Fuck, I'd never had a lover like this.

He reached for my hand and placed it on my clit, moving his own hands to my hips to push me on and off his cock. I feverishly worked my pussy while he pummeled me, my orgasm steadily building until my breath came in gasps. I clutched the sheets below for purchase and let myself go just as Forrest expanded inside me one more time, hollering through his own orgasm.

"Fuck, baby, I'm coming," he growled, rocking in and out of me, his large hands nearly encircling my waist.

I exploded again on his cock, and it was both sweet and electrifying, and amazing and precious to be close and connected to a man who was not easy to get to know. He was comfortable and trusted me, and that felt damn good.

In spite of my newfound closeness to Forrest, I'd be lying if I said I was entirely comfortable with what I knew about his—and all the guys'—profession. I mean, they'd beat around the bush about what they did but I was no dummy. It looked pretty obvious that it was borderline illegal, depending on what side you were on, and that it often included hurting or outright killing others.

As much as I enjoyed them and appreciated their taking me in, I had to say whatever they were into seemed seriously messed up. And I wanted nothing to do with it.

I mean, what the hell had they been talking about when I overheard them, with informants, crossing borders, and offshore bank accounts?

That was some James Bond kind of shit.

So, I was hitting the road. Yup, first chance I got, Ozzy and I would be out of there. I might be walking into a shit show of media thanks to *The Mating Game*, but it had to be better than hanging out with border-line criminals.

Yeah, it would suck to deal with the pesky TV cameras and reporters who were apparently still dying for my side of the 'Alessia and Mont' story, but at least I wouldn't be in close proximity to anything that smelled quasi-illegal. While my future, at the moment, was not the brightest it had ever been, I wasn't about to destroy what was left of it by hanging out with the wrong people.

No, it was time to start making some smart decisions. Look out for myself for a change.

The guys had fortunately reneged on their threat to indefinitely lock me up, so I brought Ozzy outside to teach her to play with a ball. Damn if she didn't catch on quickly to the idea of fetching, but she had no interest in bringing it back. She was more content to just run around with the thing in her mouth.

Some of us took longer than others to figure things out.

"Hey, Alessia. Whatcha up to?" Turk asked, crossing the yard toward me.

Ozzy ran up to him and nipped at his shoelaces.

"Hey, Turk. Just trying to see if we can get a game of fetch going. I'm not sure she is getting the concept."

God, his blue eyes just did me in.

"Well. Give her time."

He came over and stood so close, I could barely think.

So, I talked. Not always the best thing to do when you're nervous, but it had always worked in the past. "Whatcha up to?"

"I saw you out here and thought I'd reiterate what Forrest said about staying out of trouble."

More of *that*?

"He wasn't kidding that we won't hesitate to take out intruders. In our line of work, we sometimes have to resort to taking action first and asking questions later."

"Yeah, Turk, I think I got the message. It was pretty loud and clear, actually. But thanks."

He looked like he wanted to say something else, but thought better of it. "Okay, then. I'm off to do some work."

"See ya," I said, wrestling a soaking wet ball out of Ozzy's slimy mouth and chucking it again.

I watched him walk away, and while I was annoyed by his mini-lecture, his ass was a work of art in his khaki shorts. In fact, everything about him was perfect, from his tattered but snug T-shirt, down to his work boots.

After about the hundredth time I chucked the ball for Ozzy, she finally caught on that if she brought it back to me, I'd be able to throw it for her quicker.

As she dropped her latest retrieval at my feet, I bent down to scratch her ears.

"Hey, Ozzy," I whispered, "you wanna take a trip with me? Get the hell off this mountain?"

She jumped up, and in spite of her small size, managed to lick my face.

I took that as a *yes*.

After all the shit that had gone down since the day I'd fled my wedding, one thing that was curious was that I'd not heard a word from Mont.

I mean, the one person whom you'd think would want to have a chat with me and maybe talk me out of my rash decision to split, should have been him.

That was, if he were truly interested in marrying me, which we now knew he was not.

So, when his name showed up on my cell phone's screen, all I could think was *about time*.

"Hello, Mont."

I had debated just not answering, but to be honest, I was curious as hell to know what he wanted.

"Alessia. Good to hear your voice."

Phony motherfucker.

"Why is that, Mont? Getting tired of fucking Vanessa?"

This was going to be fun.

"I called you for a reason," he said.

"Considering I've not heard from you in so long, I hope you're calling me for a reason. What do you want?"

"I wanted to tell you I feel badly about things, and that I want to give you half my money."

Yeah, right. Was he joking?

"Go fuck yourself, Mont, and don't call me again—"

"Wait! Don't hang up, Alessia. Look. I got my half million dollars because I fulfilled my contractual obligation to the best of my ability. I got paid because your bailing wasn't my fault. But I know they're not giving you anything. I'll split mine with you, fifty-fifty."

"Why? And how do I know you're not just fucking with me, Mont?" I asked.

I had to admit, the sound of his voice made my heart race, even though I now knew he was nothing but a cowardly liar.

"I can bring you the money, Alessia. Just tell me where you are."

It was tempting. Yes, he could bring me the money, but he'd also end up a dead man. Would that be so bad?

"Mont, I'll have to meet you somewhere. And I might need a couple days to get there."

"Why? Where the hell are you?" he asked, exasperated.

"Don't worry about that. I'll let you know when I'm coming to town. And so help me, Mont, if you're fucking with me, you'll pay."

He snorted. "Yeah, yeah, tough girl. See you soon."

And he hung up.

CHAPTER 14

TURK

"Hey, Turk, need some help with dinner?" Alessia called.

Whoa. I'd thought for sure she was annoyed by my warning to stay out of trouble.

"That would be great. Will you make the salad?" I asked.

She dove into the fridge, retrieving everything she needed. "Wow, I haven't cooked in so long. If you call making a salad 'cooking,'" she laughed. "Hey, Turk," she said, putting down her chopping, "I want to apologize for being snippy earlier today. I guess you caught me at the wrong moment. I was, um, frustrated with Ozzy."

I stirred the sauce for our dinner's steaks. "It's okay.

I'm sure the last couple weeks of your life have not been your favorite."

As crabby as she'd been earlier, she sure was making up for it, and while she was always beautiful by any measure, now that she was smiling she was positively glowing.

Kind of got the old circulation flowing, if you know what I mean.

"Care for some wine, Alessia?" I asked, pouring a glass for myself.

She shook her head and continued chopping. "No thanks. Not after I overdid it last time."

Smart.

"So, Turk, I wouldn't mind doing more hiking around here. Do you have a map?"

A woman after my own heart.

"Uh, yeah. I think there's one in the living room. We sketched out most of the trails ourselves since the mountain was pretty much unexplored. But really, not sure I'd hike alone if I were you, until you learned your way around better."

She laughed. "True. I'd rather not get lost."

"I'm happy to show you a couple hikes. There are some really beautiful ones. You know, if you take that trail that's off to the left of the house, it eventually leads all the way down the mountain."

"No kidding! Hey, do you guys ever camp? I haven't in years and would love to get back into it."

"Oh, hell yeah. We camp all the time. We could get

you some gear, although maybe you can borrow some. We'll plan a trip."

She was positively thrilled. "Oh, that'd be great. I'd love that."

I had a feeling I'd love it too, being outside in the fresh air with this gorgeous, sexy woman.

Dinner was delicious, if I did say so myself.

Best of all, Alessia jumped up to help me clean the dishes.

I could see the guys were surprised too. They retired to the living room to play poker.

"Here, have some more wine," Alessia said, topping off my glass.

If I didn't know better, I'd think she was trying to get me drunk. And to be honest, she was succeeding.

"Fuck, you know how beautiful you are?" I asked, running my fingers through her dark hair when we were alone in the kitchen.

If she rebuffed me, fine, but I was at least going to try.

She looked down, her long lashes obscuring her green eyes. She shook her head. "Thank you. That's very kind of you to say."

She finally looked up at me, and when she did, I bent to kiss her. Lucky for me, her lips softened under mine, meeting me with at least as much passion as I brought.

Holding a fistful of hair, I pulled her head back and pressed harder onto her mouth, bruising her lips. I wanted to make sure she didn't forget about me anytime soon. "Let's go to your room," I whispered.

"I don't know," she said demurely.

I ran my fingers through my hair and looked around the empty kitchen while I took a deep breath. "If you don't want to, we won't. But I hope you're just fucking with me."

She ran a finger down the front of my T-shirt and didn't stop until she reached the top of my fly, which was, by now, barely concealing my hard dick.

"C'mon," she said smiling. She grabbed my hand, and we headed to her bedroom, with Ozzy right on our heels.

I slammed her door and pushed her up against it, no longer able to contain myself. With fistfuls of her hair in my hands, I kissed her until we couldn't breathe.

Without hesitation, I pulled her shirt up over her head and pounced on her perky breasts, pulling them together and burying my face in the soft flesh.

Her eyes fluttered closed as she rested her head against the door, holding on for balance.

"God baby, you have great tits," I murmured.

I reached under her skirt, pulling it up to her waist after I'd lowered her panties to her knees. God, she was fucking beautiful. A perfect, curvy hourglass shape—the kind of woman every man dreams of.

And a delicious, bare pussy.

Yet, here she was on Savage Mountain with my friends and me.

How did we get so lucky?

And how fucked was that asshole from the show who let her go?

"Turn around," I growled, pushing her against the door so I could grab fistfuls of her fleshy ass.

Smack.

"Oh!" she cried as I soothed her burning skin.

Smack.

Her bum heated up to a delightful pink as I opened my jeans and pressed my cock between her cheeks. She pushed back against me, and I nearly blew my load right there.

I pulled her over to the easy chair in the corner and sat, grabbing a condom out of my pocket. Slipping it on, I pulled her on top of me.

"You good?" I asked.

"Yeah. I am."

"Good. Then guide me into your pussy," I said.

She gripped my hard-on, directing it toward her opening, and lowered herself an inch. She gasped. "God, Turk. Your cock is big."

"Take your time, baby," I said, playing with the gorgeous tits bouncing in my face. "We're in no hurry."

And boy, wasn't that the truth. I'd had the hots for

Alessia since the moment Dash had first brought her to the house. We weren't supposed to have visitors, much less rescue a damsel in distress, but I thank god we had. As far as I was concerned, she could stay indefinitely.

She was finally fully seated on my cock, and fuck if it wasn't the goddamn sweetest sensation I'd ever known. For one, it had been far too long since I'd been with a woman, and two, women like Alessia were few and far between. I mean, how often did a guy meet someone stunning and sexy, and completely down to earth and unassuming?

Never, in my experience.

I reached for her ass and pulled her tighter, rocking her up and down on my cock with my face in her tits, while she held on to the chair back behind me.

"Turk, I'm coming," she whispered.

I sat back and watched my beautiful girl, eyes closed and lips parted as orgasm after orgasm rolled over her. She ground herself harder on me, tits and ass bouncing. Dropping her head, her hair tumbled in our faces.

It was the most fucking beautiful thing I'd ever seen.

And seconds later, I unloaded, pulling her as tightly on my exploding dick as I could without hurting her.

When we were finished, she fell forward on me like a rag doll, her head limp on my shoulder while she shuddered in my arms.

"Goddamn, baby. Incredible," I murmured.

She weakly lifted her head. "You're not so bad, yourself."

"C'mon." With her still on my lap, I stood, wrapped her legs around me, and carried her to the bed.

We lay down, and as soon as my head hit the pillow, I was out.

I opened my eyes when the sunshine blasted in the room and looked around, wondering where I was, like you do when you sleep in a new place.

Okay, I knew where I was. But why was I alone?

Alessia was nowhere to be seen. And neither was Ozzy.

I pulled on my jeans and went to the kitchen where the guys were getting coffee.

"Well, if it isn't sleeping beauty," Remy said.

"Jesus," I said, dragging my fingers through my hair. "Man, did I sleep well. What time is it?" I asked, looking around.

"Eight a.m. Late for you," Dash said. "And where's the other sleeping beauty?"

I looked from one guy to the next. "I was gonna ask you the same."

"Ha, dude, you don't have to hide that you were with her," Remy said, laughing.

Something didn't feel right. "She wasn't in bed when I woke up. And you haven't seen her either?"

We all looked at each other.

"Well, where the hell is she?" Forrest asked.

Without a word, we fanned out in all directions and began to search.

But we found nothing.

"Oh fuck, fuck, fuck," I moaned. "She'd been asking me about trails and camping and that sort of thing."

I could see we were all thinking the same thing.

"Dude, you think she took off on foot? No fucking way!" Dash said. "She couldn't do that. She doesn't know the mountain, nor does she have any experience in backwoods camping."

Forrest came running into the house. "I checked the shed. Some of our camping equipment is missing."

"Holy fuck. She thinks she can walk off the mountain. That's insane!" Dash said.

Forrest whipped around toward him. "I knew it. We should not have allowed her to stay, not even for one night. Dash, you never should have brought her here."

Dash threw his hands up in the air and narrowed his eyes. "Shut the fuck up, Forrest—"

"Okay, guys, now is not the time—"

But my peacekeeping efforts were not working.

Forrest turned to me, next. "She was asking you about getting around up here, and you didn't suspect a thing? What the fuck is wrong with you, Turk?"

Really? He was blaming *me* now?

And Remy was having none of it. He got right in Forrest's face. "Maybe if you hadn't been such a *dick* to her, she wouldn't have felt like she had to sneak off."

"All right!" Dash shouted. "Everyone shut up. I just tried to ping her phone, but I got nothing. She probably turned it off."

Forrest exploded. "And how did she know to do that, Dash? Did you share your hacking secrets with her?"

Dash just looked down at his feet and shook his head. He probably had more self restraint than any of us.

"We need to find her," I said.

"What if we just let her go?" Remy asked.

Goddammit. We needed to be focused on our upcoming summit, in preparation for our next mission. None of us really had time to go running after someone who couldn't wait to get away from us.

And yet, we had to find her. If she made one wrong move, not only could her life be in danger, but so could ours.

"Okay, guys. Let's sit down and figure out how we're going to handle this."

CHAPTER 15

ALESSIA

I'd never been one for pulling all-nighters.

But there I was.

I hated to do it, but as soon as Turk dozed off, I'd unwrapped his arms from around me and sneaked out of bed. I did glance back at him with regret, especially after the hot little session we'd just had.

But it was survival time.

He did look damn good in my bed, nude except for a tangle of sheets around one of his legs, and his bedhead hair sticking up in every direction.

Ugh. Down girl.

I tore myself away, grabbed some clothes and Ozzy,

and made my way to the shed where the guys stored their camping equipment.

The day before, when no one was around, I'd stuffed a backpack with a tent, sleeping bag, peanut butter and jelly for me, and food for Ozzy. Now, I crammed the last of my things inside, slipped my water bottles in the side pockets, and set out in the dark.

My headlamp lit the trail well, and with Ozzy, I was confident I'd scare off at least any small animals whose paths we might cross. I had a knife in my pocket, not that I'd know what to do with it if faced with danger.

I'd camped out a little in the past, but survivor woman I was not.

Turk had given me a rough idea as to which trails led down the mountain, and I felt pretty good about my prospects of making it alone.

'Course it didn't hurt that I'd also printed some maps off the computer when no one was around.

And then I'd erased my search history.

Oh, the things you learn from living with a computer geek like Dash.

I hadn't had much time to prepare, but I had to say, I'd impressed myself with how fast I'd pulled everything together. I knew it wasn't super far to get down the mountain, and if I kept my wits about me, I could be out of there in under twenty-four hours.

I was ready to start a new life. Or at least, get back to my old one. Who knew I'd miss my job at the car rental agency so much? The petty indignities, the scratchy uniform, and my quirky boss—I missed the hell out of all of it.

After about an hour walking, Ozzy started to whine. I didn't expect she'd be able to hike far, so I picked her up, tucked her into the little reusable grocery bag I'd snagged from the kitchen, and slung it around my neck.

So far, so good.

At first, it had been kind of creepy hiking in the dark and only being able to see what was directly illuminated by my headlamp. Anything beyond the light's beam was pretty much pitch black. It was sort of like walking through a tunnel.

But I calmed myself, knowing I'd planned pretty well. I'd been through worse.

Like being humiliated in front of a TV audience of millions.

Besides, I had my phone for emergencies, even though it was turned off. I didn't want to make it too easy for the guys to find me, because, of course, they'd be looking for me. Yeah, I'd picked up some of their tricks in the time I'd been with them.

After my initial nervousness, I actually began to enjoy my walk. It was so quiet, with only the occasional bird chirp when I passed too close to a nest and the sound of my hiking boots on the soft dirt trail. The air was chilly and fresh, and Ozzy was asleep in my sack, her warm little body squirming and snorting every so often against my chest.

After about three hours of hiking, I was pretty much pooped. I planned to sleep just a few hours, knowing the guys wouldn't discover I'd gone missing until the next morning—or when Turk woke up alone in my bed—whichever happened first. I'd have a good fifteen miles or so on them before they realized I was gone.

And hopefully, by that time, I'd be close to town, where I'd rent a car and be home free.

I was no camping expert, but knew enough to hike off the path to a flat spot where I was confident if the guys were looking for me, they wouldn't see me from the trail.

For the most part, I managed to get my tent up. It was lopsided, and I was pretty sure I was missing a pole, but the thing was secure enough to provide Ozzy and me some shelter.

After making myself a PB and J sandwich and giving Ozzy some dry dog food, we crawled inside and I set my watch for a few hours. I'd be up before dawn and be in town before they'd even started looking.

But of course, the moment I crawled in my sleeping bag, my mind was running a mile a minute. It's funny, when you get a few quiet moments, all the thoughts that bubble to the surface.

In this case, I was preoccupied with thoughts of the guys. With sunrise just a few hours away, Turk would be waking up in my bed, and eventually realize I'd hit the road. The guys would be furious, I just knew it, and would try to find me. But I'd be in my rental car on my way out of town before any of that happened. And I felt shitty about it.

It was no way to thank people who'd been so kind and built me up when I was feeling crappy. Hopefully, someday, I'd be able to tell them that. Maybe even return the favor.

But for now, I had to make some changes in my life, and that did not include four hunky mountain men.

By the time my thoughts calmed and I got drowsy, I had only one hour to sleep. I pulled the snoring Ozzy into a snuggle and marveled that I'd gone from being a reality TV star to sleeping in the woods.

CHAPTER 16

REMY

"Dude, we have better things to do than hunt for a wayward reality TV star," I said.

Turk shook his head. "No shit. The summit's coming like a freight train, and we're still not ready. But I don't know. I can't blame her for hitting the road, Remy. She's going through a rough patch, for sure."

Easy for Turk to say. He'd just spent the night with our beautiful young guest.

I was happy for my buddy, honestly. Spending time with a stunner like Alessia was a rare treat for us mountain guys. But she wasn't just good-looking. She was also sweet, kind, and unassuming. And she'd clearly been screwed over by that stupid TV show.

So, add naïve to that list.

Not that I'd hold it against her.

And I'd be lying if I didn't say I had hoped to have some private time with her at some point. She was just the kind of woman I craved, and having the chance to mark her in the most primitive way kept my dick hard every time I looked at her. No matter how much trouble she got herself into.

Guess I could just forget about that idea, having some one-on-one time with our gorgeous guest.

I knew she wanted to get off the mountain more than anything, which was a shame. We actually liked having her there, and not just because she was so hot. She added something, something I couldn't put into words, but that was nonetheless significant. Maybe we'd all been together too long and were getting sick of each other, but her being in the house was a breath of fresh air.

She brightened shit up.

And I thought it was kind of hot that she'd been with the other guys. It was like we were her little harem, and she was the prize.

How fucking hot was that?

Turk stopped walking and turned to me. In silence, he tapped his ear.

Not far from us, voices carried through the woods. I couldn't make out what they were saying, but whoever they were, they weren't welcome.

And they were getting closer

Turk motioned for us to step off the trail beyond the tree line so we could see who was approaching and determine how to handle the situation.

We crouched with our weapons close at hand, as we had so many times before during our missions.

The difference was, our missions were not on Savage Mountain. They were usually on the other side of the world in a foreign land. The mountain was supposed to be our sanctuary.

I pitied the person who tried to take that from us. It wouldn't end well for them. Of that, I was certain.

As their voices drew nearer and they came into view, it quickly became clear that the threat level facing us was low. Very low. Sure, these people were going to be a nuisance, but they were hardly the agents we were forever protecting ourselves against.

I jumped out of the woods and right into their faces. "Yo, guys. What do you think you're doing?" I asked.

I held my gun where it was not menacing but could still be clearly seen. Which had the desired effect.

"Whoa, dude. What's with the gun?" asked a young guy balancing a bulky video camera on his shoulder. He took a big step back.

His buddy, a short guy carrying a large microphone, wasn't watching and ran smack into his friend who'd just stopped short.

And his face turned dead white.

"Holy shit," he said.

Turk emerged from the woods after I'd fully made my impression.

I was wishing *I* had a camera, because the looks on their faces were too great to miss.

They backed up a few feet just as Turk and I took a couple steps toward them.

The one with the camera held up his free hand. "Hey, man, we're not looking for any trouble. We were sent here by our show."

Turk cocked his head. "And what show would that be?"

They looked at each other.

"Um, *The Mating Game*. Our producer sent us here to shoot some footage. And to look for one of our contestants."

It had probably been just a matter of time before some numbskulls from the show stormed the mountain.

The one with the mic leaned close to his friend. "I told them this was private property. We're trespassing. Let's get the hell out of here."

"No shit, dude. Didn't know we'd be stumbling across guys like this."

"Hey, man," the short guy said, "we didn't mean to disturb you. We'll just be on our way, okay?"

They turned to go.

"Hey," I said.

They stopped without looking up.

"Not so fast."

They turned around, terrified.

I felt a little badly scaring the shit out of these guys, but they needed to learn a lesson they could take back to their 'show.'

"Come with us," Turk said.

He led the way, and I followed our visitors, back to the cabin.

If our business partners who were participating in the summit knew our security had almost been breached, that could be the end of our missions, not to mention, potentially, the end of our lives. It was a cold reality of the work we did that the services we provided were more valuable than we as individuals were. Our skills were in high demand, but if push came to shove, we were expendable.

It was the price of dancing with the devil, as I was told my first day in training.

"Okay. You assholes sit right here," I said, gesturing at the kitchen table. "You want water or something?"

They looked at each other again and nodded.

"Um, yeah. Please," the short one said.

Turk poured them tall glasses, and I could swear I saw the tall one sniff it before he took a sip.

Someone'd been watching too much TV.

I took a seat right in front of them and placed my hands on my knees.

"Okay, fellas. Tell us where you're from, how you found us, and what you were up to," I said.

They both gulped.

The tall one started babbling. "Look, we're sorry, dude. Our boss made us come here to look for a contestant from our reality show. We'll leave and just tell everyone we found nothing. But please, don't hurt us."

Not that I could blame them, but they clearly thought we were murderous maniacs. Best to keep them a little scared.

"Why'd you think your contestant was here?" Turk asked.

They looked at each other again.

"I suggest you tell us the truth."

The short one's eyes opened wide. "Yeah, man. I guess they tracked her phone or something. They figured she was somewhere around here. Billy and Mont said—"

But he was elbowed in the ribs before he could continue.

He glared at his buddy. "Dude? You're protecting them? They sent us up here, and we could end up dead." He lowered his voice and leaned closer to him. "Look at these guys. We're no match for them."

I had to hold back my laughter

"Why does the show want this person so much?" I asked.

"Because, she was really popular and brought in lots of viewers. People loved her. And lots of viewers equal lots of advertisers. And that means a shit-ton of money."

It was always about money, wasn't it?

I gestured at Turk, and we stepped away from the guys to confer.

My brother Cap probably would have shot them in the ass.

"What do you think?" Turk asked.

"I say just scare the shit out of them and send them on their way,"

"Well, I think we've already accomplished that, Remy."

The short one had sweat dripping down his temples. "Look, man, we don't want any trouble. Just let us go and we won't say anything. We won't tell anyone you're living up here. We swear."

"Okay. We can do that. But first give us your IDs. Then we'll take you back to town. If you ever show up here again, or any of your associates for that matter, we can't promise you'll be safe."

He gulped. "I understand. And promise. We won't be back."

On the way down the mountain, the two guys, now in the back seat, jabbered about the hornets' nest they'd run into.

"Fuckers don't pay me enough to put my life on the line," one of them said.

"Totally. I'd like to throw this camera out the window right now. Teach them a lesson about putting us in harm's way. Dude, there's a reason I'm on a reality

TV crew and not a news crew. I don't want to die young."

When we got to town, we dropped them at their car, certain we'd done about as good a job as possible at scaring the shit out of them.

"Okay. What now?" Turk asked.

"Since we're here in town and rid of those knuckle-heads, let's look around real quick. But I'll bet Alessia's still on the mountain somewhere. Probably lost, hungry, and cold."

And I didn't like the idea of our girl being any of those things. She deserved to be in a comfortable, warm home with people who cared about her.

Like us guys on Savage Mountain.

CHAPTER 17

ALESSIA

I threw my pack and camping equipment in the trunk, got some water for Ozzy, and peeled out of the car rental lot.

Even before I'd gotten there, I knew they'd never let me rent a car without a credit card, and since dickhead Mont had shut mine off, I had to think fast. I called Lady, who talked to the agent I was dealing with. They took her card information, and I was good to go.

The whole thing took less than ten minutes.

And now that my cell was turned on again, I went through all the messages the guys from the cabin had left me.

Dash: Um, Alessia, I guess you've turned your phone off because you know we can trace it…

Forrest: Alessia, I wish you hadn't taken off this way. I… I don't know what to say…

Turk: Hey babe, we had such a good time last night. Why'd you leave? I'm coming to look for you so stay safe…

Remy: Jesus, sweetie, I thought things were going okay. Would you please get in touch so I at least know you're all right…

Well. Now I felt like crap. But I couldn't let my feelings for the guys hold me back. I'd been a pleaser all my damn life, and it was time to stop.

Now.

But they were so damned amazing…

If I'd had a little more sense about looking out for myself, I wouldn't be in a car racing across two states to collect money from my ex-fiancé.

No, I'd be safely ensconced in my predictably boring world of renting cars and hanging out with Lady, chasing cheap happy hours and gossiping about hot customers.

No one would know who I was, and no one would care to.

But I'd made my bed.

The alarm on my watch hadn't actually woken me that morning in the tent—Ozzy had, growling at something. It had probably only been a deer, but the crunching outside our tent was promptly scared off by one little bark from my miniature bodyguard.

I knew I loved that dog.

And since we were both awake, I packed everything up and we continued our trek down the mountain, making it to town before the sun was even up. I had to admit, I'd enjoyed my little camping adventure and was sorry it was so short.

But I could always go camping again. Maybe even bring Lady next time.

With my rented wheels, I got the hell out of town, driving twenty minutes to the nearest, nondescript motel. I got a room and Ozzy and I went back to sleep for a few hours.

And don't you know, I dreamt about the guys.

At the diner where we'd agreed to meet, Montgomery leaned back in the booth where he'd been waiting for me, smiling like he'd won the lottery.

Smug fuck.

"Well, if it isn't my almost-wifey. You look exhausted. And I thought you were off on a nice little vacation."

His face, which I'd once found so handsome, was now nothing but vulgar deceitfulness. How had I never noticed the bags under his eyes, his thinning hair, and his tacky waxed eyebrows?

Had he always been like that, and I'd just not noticed?

It was amazing, the things you could overlook when you were under pressure.

He reached for Ozzy's furry head. "You got a puppy. How cute. Let me pet her."

I pulled her out of his reach, but not before she growled and nipped at him.

Good dog.

I kissed her on the head. "Looks like she's a much better judge of character than I am."

He rolled his eyes. "So, where have you been? I was worried about you."

Okay, that one had me burst out laughing.

"I'd tell you. But then I'd have to kill you." I sat back in the booth with my arms crossed, lips pressed together, Ozzy glaring.

He leaned across the table and tried to reach for my hand, but I grabbed for the coffee the waitress had just poured.

He sighed and pulled back, dejected. "Look, I'm sorry. Sorry about everything. I didn't mean for things to go this way. Everything got so... complicated."

"I guess being honest and telling the truth are complicated for some people."

I wanted to throw my hot coffee at him. But I wanted my money even more.

He played with his fingernails for a moment. Was that shame I saw cross his face?

No. Not possible.

He took a deep breath, puffing up his chest.

I'd never realized how scrawny he was until I started spending time with the mountain men. 'Course, they'd make anyone look small.

Was I missing them?

No time for that, now.

He took a deep breath. "It started out kind of innocent. Billy forced me to choose *you*, even though I wanted Vanessa. Nothing personal, it's just that I had a great connection with her. Still do." He looked at me like he was afraid I would hit him. "I liked you, Alessia, but really, we weren't meant to be together. I'm sorry I hurt you."

Vanessa *was* more his type. Good-looking, shallow, money-hungry…

"Whatever, Mont. Keep going with the story."

"So, Billy told me I could be with Vanessa later, but that if I chose you, the show would pay both of us a shit-ton of money." He put his head in his hands. "I wanted to tell you so many times, but they wouldn't let me. They didn't think you'd go through with the wedding if you knew it was all staged."

"They were right." I leaned onto the table between us, confident he wouldn't try to touch me again.

"By the way, I saw Billy and you on TV, laughing your asses off at me. As if I'd done something wrong. As if I'd been the liar. So *fuck you*. Fuck *all of you*. I want my money, Mont, and then I'll be on my way. You all got your prize, and now I want mine." I pushed my empty coffee cup away and looked at my watch for emphasis.

He threw some money on the table and stood. "All right. Let's go."

"Where?" I cradled Ozzy in my lap and didn't budge.

He threw his arms up in the air. "I can't give you the money right here."

"Go get me a money order. I'll wait here."

"All right. Sure you don't want to come with?"

Why did he keep looking out the diner window?

"Nope. I'm good. I'll have a nice leisurely breakfast, and by the time I'm done, you'll be back with my check. And you will have alleviated some of the guilt that is surely keeping you up at night."

Yeah, right.

"Um. Okay. See you in a bit." He headed for the door.

I waved the waitress over. "Good morning. I'll have two eggs over easy, and pancakes with a side of sausage—"

"My darling, Alessia!" a cheerful voice behind me called.

A male voice.

A very familiar male voice.

"What the *fuck* are you doing here, Billy?" I jumped to my feet, and bless her heart, Ozzy barked and lunged.

The poor waitress wasn't sure what to do, so she stepped back with her pad and pen in hand, looking from one of us to the other.

I stepped toward Billy. "What's going on here?"

I looked out the diner window and saw Mont sitting in the passenger seat of a van.

Mont didn't have a van.

Before I could even turn back to Billy, he had ahold of my arm and began pulling me toward the door.

Ozzy went flying out of my arms, running around us and barking in a frenzy.

"Don't mind us, miss," Billy said to the waitress, "just a little husband and wife misunderstanding."

She took another step backward. I couldn't blame her.

But I wasn't going down that easy. "What are you doing? Get off me, you asshole."

He half-dragged me out of the diner, with Ozzy nipping at his heels.

"I just need to talk to you for a bit. C'mon."

We were headed straight for the van, where Mont watched from the front seat with a mixture of curiosity and horror on his face.

What the fuck? Was I being kidnapped or something?

Billy pulled open the back door of the van. "Get in," he said as he shoved me.

And if that weren't bad enough, he left Ozzy in the parking lot.

"Hey, let me out. Let me out of here," I screamed, pounding on the door that slammed in my face and was locked from the outside. "What about my dog?"

I scooted up to the van's partition window, just behind the front seat, and pounded on it.

"What are you doing? Where are we going? And you left my dog behind, you fuckers. Get my dog!"

"No can do, pretty girl. And forget about that nasty little dog." Billy started the van while Mont shifted uncomfortably and looked out the window.

Oh, my god. I frantically looked for a window in the back of the van, but there were none. I couldn't see Ozzy, but I could hear her barking up a storm. Would someone pick her up? Would I ever get her back?

In my panic, I realized that in all the commotion, Billy had grabbed my bag and it was now in the front seat with them.

These guys were certifiably crazy.

I took a deep breath. It wouldn't pay to lose my shit.

"Hey guys," I said calmly, "can you at least let me call Lady? She was expecting my call and will be worried."

Mont turned in his seat. "Lady? That hick friend of yours?" He snorted. "You girls just love those polyester uniforms, don't you?"

It was a good thing there was a window between us, because I really think I could have killed him with my bare hands.

"Give me my phone, asshole."

Billy pulled into traffic and waved his hand in the

air. "Give it to her, Mont. Let her call her friend. And that better be the only person you call, Alessia."

Mont began fishing through my bag.

I took a deep, calming breath. "So tell me, what are you guys doing? I mean, you can't go around kidnapping people. In case you weren't aware, it's against the law."

"Look, Alessia," Billy said, looking at me in the rearview mirror, "I just wanted to talk some sense into you. We're gonna go someplace neutral to have a little chat. I want you to come back to the show. I'll make it worth your while."

I shook my head. "Are you kidding? I don't want anything to do with that goddamn show."

A forced smile grew across his face, then morphed into an expression of anger. He slammed his hand on the steering wheel, scaring the shit out of me.

"What you don't understand, you simpleton," he yelled, "is that my career depends on this show. If I don't get the network the ratings they want, I lose my job. And right now, all anyone who watches *The Mating Game* wants to see is *you*. So, you *will* go on the show."

Okay. The guy was delusional. He thought I could save his dumbass show, so he kidnaps me and thinks I'll go along with everything.

Was Mont equally as delusional?

I scrolled through the contacts on my phone and stopped on Dash. "Hi, Lady. It's me, Alessia," I said when he answered.

"Alessia? Where are you?"

"Yeah, it's been really busy. But I expect to be home soon. How's work?"

"You can't talk?" he asked.

I laughed. "Nope. No way can you come visit. But I can't wait to see you, girlfriend. It's been way too long."

"Leave your phone on. We're coming to get you," he said and hung up.

"Okay, sweetie," I continued, talking to a dead line, "I'll let you know as soon as I'm in town. It should be soon." And then, for Billy's benefit I added, "You know, I might be going back on the show. Billy says they really, really want me. What? I can't hear you. You're breaking up."

Billy looked at me in the rearview mirror again, so I rolled my eyes dramatically.

"Disconnected. Darn phones."

"So where have you been all this time, since you left me at the altar?" Mont laughed.

"Well… that's kind of complicated…"

I stalled, hoping they wouldn't see me sending Dash a text message about Ozzy.

Mont gave me one of his smiles, which I'd once thought was genuine but now knew was nothing but contemptuous.

"Fine. We have a long drive ahead of us. Why don't you start telling us your story right now?"

CHAPTER 18

DASH

"Oh, hey, I think I know you!" I hollered after the sweaty, spray-on-tan guy emerging from the gas station men's room.

Billy's eyes widened as he pulled himself up to full height and proudly puffed out his chest. "Oh, hello. You probably know me from television."

I snapped my fingers. "That's right. You're on TV. Now, let me think. What show would I have seen you on?"

He waited to see if I could come up with it. "*The Mating Game*," he offered impatiently.

"*That's* right." I clapped my hands with enthusiasm. "What's your name, man? I'm Dash."

I extended my hand for a shake.

"Billy. Billy Brent."

"Right! Yours is the show with the fine young thing who left the guy at the altar?"

He nodded enthusiastically and looked over my shoulder. "Yes, can you believe that? The guy was just devastated, but you know how relationships are. Tricky enough, but when the whole world is watching… well, it's a different story. But she'll be back on soon to explain everything that went down. It'll be the most-watched show of the year."

Not if I had anything to do with it.

"I'll look forward to that." I was dying to punch him in his smarmy face.

He looked over my shoulder. "Hey, I gotta get rolling. I have some friends in the car waiting for me."

"Oh, right." I started walking with him. "Hey, what was the name of the woman on the show? You know, the one the bachelor chose to marry?"

He started walking faster, clearly not happy to have a curious fan on his tail. "Her name is Alessia."

As we neared the van, I saw Mont, the douchebag who'd been making fun of Alessia on the recent TV show, in the front seat.

"No way," I said. "Is that… is that the star of the show? Montgomery Langton?"

Billy was clearly getting irritated he hadn't been able to shake me.

"Dude, I loved you on *The Mating Game*." I yanked

the passenger door open and extended my hand for a shake.

That's when I saw Alessia through the partition. I grabbed Mont and pulled him out of the van. He went flying to the ground, and Forrest emerged from our truck and went after Billy.

"Open it." I pointed to the back of the van.

Mont crawled to his feet and dusted himself off. "Fuck you, man."

I usually gave people two chances. But I was feeling cranky and decided this guy only deserved one. So, I slugged him in the nose with a closed fist.

His screams attracted the attention of the others in the gas station, but I didn't care. A couple people rolled up their windows and got the hell out of there. The cashier locked the doors and ducked behind the counter.

"My nose, my nose," he shouted as blood gushed between the fingers he pressed to his face.

With him out of commission, I opened the van door myself, and Alessia came flying into my arms.

"Dash! Oh, my god. Thank you for coming for me." She threw her arms around my neck, and I had to say, she felt damn good.

When she released me, she glanced around at the carnage we'd created. With Mont writhing on the ground, she went after Billy.

Who was unfortunately restrained by Forrest and couldn't defend himself.

Alessia ran toward him and kicked him in the balls with what looked like every bit of strength she had in her body.

Billy joined his friend on the ground, where they were both experiencing pain they'd probably never felt before.

And Alessia apparently wasn't done. She started kicking both guys wherever her hiking boot could make contact with their bodies.

Christ, I'd have to remember never to piss her off. She was lethal.

"I'll never be on your show you fucking assholes," she screamed.

Forrest had to pull her off the guys. "C'mon. We need to get out of here."

"Wait." She ran to the front seat of the van, where she retrieved her bag.

"Alessia, grab the car keys," I shouted as I proceeded to puncture their tires with a large knife.

We jumped in our truck, and Forrest peeled out of the gas station. When I looked back, the two losers were still on the ground holding their respective injuries. They'd probably be there for a while, and when they did get up off the ground, they wouldn't get far without their ignition key and their tires flattened.

Alessia leaned over the seat and grabbed my arm. "My dog. We have to get Ozzy. They left her at the diner. And my rental car is there. It has your camping equipment in it."

I called Turk and Remy. "Guys, it's Dash. You find the dog yet? Okay, cool. Yeah, we'll see you back at the cabin."

I turned to Alessia. "The guys got Ozzy. She's fine."

Our girl gasped with relief, and her eyes opened wide, allowing several big, fat tears to roll down her face.

"I... I'm... so sorry," she sputtered.

Her face crumpled, and she buried her head in her hands.

I'm not sure I'd ever seen anyone cry like she began to. I guess she was processing the shit show that had been her life in recent weeks and months, and it all caught up with her at that very moment.

I felt for her. I really did. She'd lost a lot.

But gained a lot, too. She just didn't realize it yet.

It was time to have a talk with our girl. She needed to know that what she was up against was far more dire than a reality show with a crazy producer and cast.

Turk and Remy had found Ozzy hiding under a bush in the diner parking lot. She jumped right in their car and when they arrived back at the cabin, she made a flying leap for Alessia, licking her face all over.

After getting cleaned up, we all convened in the living room.

"Guys, I just want to say how sorry I am to have put

you through what happened today. I really thought I could just get my money from Mont and disappear without bothering anybody." She looked around the living room from one of us to the other, clearly hoping for us to forgive her.

But it wasn't that simple.

Remy leaned forward, elbows on his knees as he sat facing her. "We've decided to share a bit more with you than we have until now, so you understand who we are and how it impacts you."

"Okay." She sat straight and attentive, still working on getting back into our good graces.

"You know we're all former military, special ops, now private security contractors."

She nodded. "Yeah, Remy. But I don't know much more than that."

He nodded. "That's okay. So what it means is that we're hired to do jobs that either militaries or governments don't want to do themselves."

"Do you know what that means, Alessia?" I asked.

She shook her head, *no*.

"We sometimes have to find people, or assets, that are very hard to locate. And to do that, we have to do some things that are… on the unsavory side—"

Alessia held up her hands. "I get it. And I don't want to know more."

"Fine. That's fine. You don't need the gory details. But what you do need to understand is how this impacts *you*," Remy continued. "Because of some of the jobs we do, we have enemies. We have to keep low profiles. Some of them would love nothing more than to cut off our heads with machetes."

Alessia's face rumpled in disgust.

I wouldn't have put it that way, but Remy had never been the most diplomatic guy.

"Your associating with us means you're a target, too," he continued.

"What? Why?" She looked around the room in confusion.

It was to be expected.

"Any folks after us will assume you're part of our operation. These people shoot first, and never ask questions."

She nodded slowly. "Okay. Then, I'll leave. What I was actually trying to do yesterday. Well, before I was kidnapped, anyway."

"Well, that's part of the problem. You can't just take off like nothing ever happened, as if you'd never spent time with us up here in the cabin. You need to be prepared. Learn how to handle firearms and other weapons in case you need to defend yourself."

She fell back against the sofa. "Are you kidding? No way!"

"It's a precaution. But we take precautions pretty seriously. That's why we're still alive," I added.

Forrest chimed in. "It might not seem like it, Alessia, but we like having you here. We really do. But we want you to be safe. One weak link, and everyone is in danger."

She frowned. "I'd hardly say I was a weak link."

"Well, you are. Or rather, you were. Now that you know the implications of staying here, we're all better off," he added.

"You know, Alessia, you can stay here as long as you want," I added.

"But Dash, I thought I was intruding."

"Initially that was true, but... well, we've grown attached to you." I looked around the room, and the guys nodded.

But Alessia laughed. "Oh yeah, right. You like me just like Mont liked me, huh?"

Okay, the woman had some trust issues. I probably would, too, if I'd been dicked over like she had.

Turk jumped in. "Alessia, we have a summit coming up. A very important, very high security meeting with some of our business partners. That includes other operatives and the clients who hire us. People are coming from all over the world. It's in four weeks, and we need everything to go smoothly. People are going to want to know what you are doing here and what your role is."

"Well, maybe I could help in some way?" she asked hopefully.

Now, she was thinking.

"We want to find a role for you, if you're open to it."

"Well, while we're figuring that out, maybe we have time for some fun?" she asked wickedly.

Holy shit. Did she really just say that?

I walked over and pulled her to her feet. I couldn't sit there any longer just admiring her long, shapely legs. And other things.

I needed more, and I was hoping she did, too.

I kissed the side of her neck as a warm-up, and her deep sigh revealed her pleasure, egging me on.

There was a lot more where that came from.

She looked around, beckoning all the guys, and Remy was the first at her side. We each kissed her while she ran her fingers through our hair, the stresses of the day quickly relegated to the background, along with the satisfaction of knowing that happiness was always the best revenge.

CHAPTER 19

ALESSIA

A massive thunderclap shook the cabin, and the lights flickered. The guys were unfazed, but poor Ozzy whimpered from my room. One of the guys went to fetch her, wrapping her in a blanket and bringing her to the living room where Dash and Remy were kissing me.

One big, happy family.

I arched my neck to give Remy better access. "Hey, what if the power goes out?"

Turk was busy removing my T-shirt and shorts. "We have a generator."

Oh, right. Of course.

The house shook again, and the drizzle that had

been wetting the cabin's windows turned torrential, the way water drenched your windshield in a carwash until you couldn't see out.

Someone lit candles. Not sure who. My brain was thinking only of pleasure.

Then, I was blindfolded.

And the effect was magical.

There I was. Horrible, scary weather outside—I mean, what if it had rained like that when I was camping?—but safe indoors in a mountain cabin with four gorgeous, built men who wanted their way with me.

And didn't seem to mind sharing.

It was so freaking hot, especially knowing how we'd bested Billy and Mont.

A great day all around.

I wanted the guys at least as much as they wanted me. I craved release and affection after the hurt I'd been going through. I was ready to start healing.

And let my new friends know how much I enjoyed them.

I fell to my knees and grabbed the first cock thrust in my face. I'd been with two guys once before, when Lady had bailed on a double date. It was nothing special. Just kind of weird and awkward.

This time would be different, no doubt about it.

I licked precum off someone's hard dick, then closed my lips around the swollen head. Whoever I was servicing—I had no idea, thanks to the blindfold— sucked his breath hard, his thighs shaking as he stood.

My thong panty was slipped below my ass, and hands kneaded my cheeks, opening and closing them and exposing my most private parts. Something about not being able to see anything obliterated any self-consciousness I might have once felt. Instead, my confidence soared. I felt sexy and powerful, thanks to the murmurs of approval surrounding me.

Still on my knees, someone guided me forward until my hands met the floor. The cock in my mouth popped out and was replaced with a new one.

"God, baby, I love how you suck me," Remy murmured.

Well, *now* I knew whose cock I had in my mouth.

But what I didn't know was who was running their tongue over my asshole, tormenting me with an unfamiliar sensation.

That I liked. A lot.

I took Remy's cock all the way, his head banging against the back of my throat. With a deep breath, I was able to hold off on gagging until he pushed into my face as a surprise fuck. Tears streamed from my eyes and I sputtered but got right back to sucking as soon as I'd recovered.

It was amazing how the guys had come for me when I was in trouble. They'd shown me what loyalty meant—something never displayed by the creeps on *The Mating Game*. And now, they were showing me love.

Shit. Did I just say *love*?

Four pairs of hands roamed over my body, burning me with sensation. I wanted to be taken and fucked until I couldn't talk or walk.

Christ, what was happening to me?

I sucked the cock in my mouth harder and found another on my right side that I took in hand and slowly jerked. Someone was playing with my tits, and the tongue on my ass burrowed into me until I felt myself opening up.

Remy, fucking my face, exploded in my mouth. His groans dwarfed the screams of the storm outside and were followed by a string of expletives that made the other guys chuckle.

Someone's warm breath was next to my ear, but it wasn't until he began to speak that I realized it was Turk.

"You good, honey? You feeling good?" he asked, smoothing his hand over my back.

I nodded. "Yeah. I'm good," was all I could manage.

"Well, how's this feel?"

He slipped a finger in my ass. And I had to admit, it felt awesome.

I nodded as another cock rubbed against my cheek. I opened my mouth obediently.

"Tell me if you want me to stop," he said.

I was so wound up, I took the cock as deep as I could, holding it against the back of my throat until another gag reflex subsided.

Behind me, there was pressure on my asshole, and then a stretching and burning sensation.

"Push out a bit, baby," Turk said while massaging my ass cheeks.

Someone else had their hand on my clit, making gentle circular motions.

Was I in heaven? Because it sure as hell felt like it.

Turk stretched me further and before I knew it, I was full of his cock, coming like I never had before.

Ass sex. Who knew?

I let the cock fall out of my mouth and began to moan.

"Fuck me, Turk. It's so good," I murmured.

"Oh, oh," he hollered as he plunged deep inside me one last time.

And just as he did, he pulled out and spurted all over my back.

I collapsed on the floor in front of our roaring fire, too weak to remove my blindfold.

Someone picked me up and carried me to bed. Last thing I knew was that Ozzy had jumped up and worked her way into my armpit, where she got back to her snoring.

While it had been beyond satisfying to see Billy and Mont have the shit beaten out of them, not to mention their car disabled, I sure didn't end up any closer to getting my money from the show.

I hadn't started out doing *Mates* for the money. I mean, I never thought I'd get past the first episode or two before being booted off. I just didn't have the game —or glamour—of the other girls. They seemed to know shit I didn't, like how to manipulate each other, the people running the show, and good old Mont himself. They knew how to dress, do their hair and makeup, walk, talk, and act, not to mention gain the almighty influencer following on social media. Some of them had tens of thousands of followers.

In some ways, I suppose Mont was as much a victim as I. He frequently looked like a deer in the headlights, which at the time, I'd found endearing. On the surface, it probably sounds like fun to have twenty attractive women throwing themselves at you, but in reality, it was probably a stressful pain in the ass.

Especially when the show's producers were controlling your every move. They honestly had no more interest in Mont's well-being than than mine.

I'd signed on in the beginning because it looked kind of fun. That's what everyone told me, anyway.

I'd caved like the idiot pleaser that I was.

Fuck that.

As the weeks passed, I was as puzzled as anyone that I was still on the show. I'd planned on being back at work after just a couple weeks.

In fact, I'd even considered dropping out early on.

Our contracts permitted us to do that under certain circumstances—we'd just have to forfeit any compensation. But I didn't care. I thought the whole thing was stupid, and the other girls on the show were mostly a bunch of bitches. The only two I thought were cool were jettisoned right away.

So, when I let on that I wanted to bail, well, you'd have thought I'd just murdered someone. I mean, the producers FREAKED. When their begging to stay didn't change my mind, they resorted to threats in order to twist my arm. Lawsuits, crap like that.

Which should have been proof enough that I needed to get out of that shit show.

And then Mont took me aside for a chat. Now that I look back, I'm sure it was at the producers' urging—but he told me he'd feel awful if I left. That he wanted to see where things might go between us.

That he really liked me.

Thanks, buddy.

But I stuck around, ignoring the little signs around me that something was off—the most obvious being that if they were getting rid of the down to earth nerdy girls, why the hell were they keeping me?

Well, now I had answers to all my questions.

Yay.

The fancy parties, limo rides, and gorgeous clothes were fun. So were the paid-for trainers and nice food and wine.

But if I had it to do all over again?

Hell no.

Although the debacle did enable my meeting the mountain guys.

The mountain guys I'd slept with just last night. All *four*.

Holy crap. Wait until I told Lady.

Actually, not sure I'd tell her I'd been with four guys. That might be a bit much, even for her horny approach to life.

It blew my mind that they wanted me to stick around. They liked having me there. They liked *me*.

Imagine. What a concept.

But sticking around just wasn't possible. Even though the mountain was amazing, and the guys were stuff most women only ever dream of or see in magazines.

I had *shit* to do.

Like get back to my job and continue saving money to continue my education.

'Course, if I'd gotten that little windfall from the show, I could go back to school right away, and not have to worry about making money for a year or two.

Yeah. I still wanted my damn money.

"Hey, Forrest, whatcha doing?" I asked.

He snapped his laptop shut. "Hi. Just some things for the summit."

I plopped down next to him on the sofa. "Secret stuff? Is that why you closed your computer?"

A smile swept across his face, highlighting those damn dimples that made my heart race. He pushed his hair back, showing off his neck tattoo.

Yowsa.

"There are some things we can't share with you. You know that. It's for your own safety, as well as ours."

I wish Forrest liked me half as much as he liked his rules. Even Ozzy wasn't sure about him. She sat in front of us on the floor, like she was my bodyguard, waiting for a reason to pounce.

I slapped his knee. "I was kidding. I actually don't want to know any of the gory details."

I looked around the room and took a deep breath. "But there *is* one important thing I wanted to ask you about."

CHAPTER 20

FORREST

I rapped on the outbuilding door—the one Alessia had stumbled on that had gotten her into so much trouble. "Dash, we need you to work your magic on someone."

A small smile crept across his face. "Are you asking what I think you're asking?"

I shrugged. "We have the technology. Why not?"

"Why not, indeed." He cracked his knuckles for emphasis and began tapping on his keyboard. "Do you have all the required identifiers?"

"Got 'em right here," I said, showing him a note on my phone that contained all of Montgomery Langton's vitals.

"Alessia know about this?" Dash asked.

I nodded. "Of course. She came to me, asking if we could help get her money from the creep you beat the shit out of the other day."

Dash smiled proudly. "Oh, yeah. You should have seen him, on the ground, blood pouring out of his nose. Poor bastard."

I slapped him on the back. "Yeah, you seem really sorry."

He rolled his eyes and laughed. "Give me some time to get the wheels in motion."

"Sounds good. Be careful."

"I always am." He turned back to his PC, fading into his information surveillance mode.

Some might call it espionage. Either way, it worked for me.

A few hours later, Dash called me back over to his office.

He high-fived me when I got there.

"Dude, this must be one of the easiest jobs I've ever done. The guy's stuff had only the minimum security measures in place."

"Well, that makes sense. He'd have no reason to have that shit. He's not in our business," I said.

He nodded, tapping on his keyboard and logging into some secret app that only he could access. "Right. Sometimes, I just forget how vulnerable civilians are and how they have no clue about it."

Looking over his shoulder at the computer monitor, I asked, "So what'd you find?"

"Along with access to his accounts, I got into his phone. Listen."

How are you feeling baby? a female voice asked.

Fucking horrible. Alessia's henchmen did a job on my nose. I'm in agony even with painkillers. I could kill those fuckers.

I recognized the voice as Mont's. The woman must have been the secret girlfriend. I had to stifle a laugh at the sound of his nasally voice. His nose must have been packed with cotton.

Well, is she coming back to the show?

Vanessa, I told you she wouldn't come back. I also told Billy she wouldn't come back. But that fucker wouldn't listen, and now my face is busted.

At least you don't have to give her any money.

Ha. Like I was going to do that, anyway. I only said that to lure her.

Well, you have to get a safe deposit box. I don't like having all that cash Billy paid you in the house.

Just relax Vanessa. Everything will be fine.

"Holy shit," I said. "He has cash in his house? I bet Alessia would be interested in hearing that. Did they talk about anything else?"

Dash nodded. "Yeah. They said Billy has money in his house, too. Do these idiots have any idea how they're giving away the store?"

"Apparently not. I think the last thing on their minds is that their phones might be tapped."

"Probably doesn't happen too much in the circles they run with." I burst out laughing. Couldn't help myself.

Those losers had no idea what they were up against.

But no one really knew what they were up against when it came to us guys.

Dash and I headed back to the house. "Alessia!"

She looked up from where she was playing catch with Ozzy. Or, I should say, *trying* to play catch. Poor little puppy was still having trouble with the concept.

"Hi, guys." Flushed, she was out of breath from running, her face glistening with the lightest layer of perspiration.

Christ, she was even adorable when she was running around with a dog. And I wanted her.

Badly.

But that would have to wait until later.

"Hey, Alessia, Forrest and I have some info to share. Do you have a sec to talk?" Dash asked.

She put her hands on her hips. "Well, I don't know. I really don't like my doggy training sessions to be interrupted. But for you guys—I guess I could make an exception." She laughed, her green eyes glinting in the mid-day sun.

"Alessia," I said, "what do you think of taking a road trip?"

~

An hour outside LA, Turk navigated through the area's famously horrendous traffic. But it had no adverse impact on our moods. There was something about LA —when the first palm trees come into view, and if you're lucky, the iconic Hollywood sign along with it— traffic jams were a lot less painful.

In the back seat, where we sat, Alessia looked like a kid in a candy store. She couldn't stop smiling, and grabbed for my hand.

Remy, in the passenger seat, pulled out his phone and dialed. "Hey, Dash, we're just now arriving."

Dash and the puppy had remained behind at the cabin.

Remy swiped his phone closed. "Okay, he's tracking the guys without any trouble."

Alessia shook her head. "That's so wild, that you can do that."

Turk laughed. "We can do way more than that, sweetie."

I rummaged around in my backpack and handed her a few items. "Can you put these things on, please?"

She took the wig and sunglasses I gave her, turning them over in her hands as if she'd never seen anything like them.

"I'm not wearing this thing, Forrest." She held the wig up between two fingers.

She could be such a pain in the ass. Which, I suppose, was part of the reason I liked her.

"Actually, you are going to wear *both* of these items, and you need to put them on right now."

She rolled her eyes. "You have got to be kidding. C'mon, Forrest—"

"No. I am not. We can't risk anyone identifying you."

She looked at me like I was crazy, and then twisted her hair up and pulled the short blonde wig tight over her head.

Remy turned from the front seat. "Hey, you look good as a blonde."

She rolled her eyes. "Thanks, Remy."

"No one will identify her now," he said, turning back in his seat.

She held her hand out. "Sunglasses."

Remy was right. With the wig and sunglasses, she was virtually unidentifiable.

Perfect.

She ran her fingers through the wig and looked at herself in a small makeup mirror. "Maybe it's not so bad, this being incognito."

Turk laughed from the front seat. "Guys, sounds like someone might actually enjoy our line of business. Do we have a new recruit on our hands?"

Alessia shook her head. "No way. But I appreciate the thought. So, what are the plans, anyway?"

"Tonight, we relax. Check into the hotel, have a nice dinner. Tomorrow we move on our targets," I said.

"Oh, my god," Alessia laughed. "That sounds so sinister."

I ruffled her blonde wig. "Sorry, baby. Old habits die hard."

And my old habits weren't the only thing that were hard.

I'd booked us into the penthouse suite of LA's swankiest hotel. All three of us guys, as well as Alessia, had our own bedrooms. But I couldn't deny I was hoping Alessia might be interested in sharing.

I know the other guys were, too.

Poor Dash, home alone. Well, he did have Ozzy.

After an amazing dinner, where I could swear Alessia was purposely teasing the shit out of us, we returned to our suite and ordered champagne for our girl and bourbon for us guys.

Turned out Alessia wanted bourbon, too.

Now *that* was *hot*.

As we sat around the living room of our suite, Alessia insisted on serving our drinks. When she was done, she put on some sexy music and started swaying. I'd never seen her so loose and happy.

Her long black dress was perfect with her blonde wig.

I leaned back in my chair like the other guys, admiring the view.

"Are you taking that off?" I asked, pointing at the wig.

She shook her head, flipping the hair back and forth over her face. "Not yet. I'm getting a kick out of feeling like a different person. It's liberating."

I could understand the need for escape. That's basically how I ended up on Savage Mountain. Too much ugliness in the field had gotten into every pore of my body. But I was slowly healing. The mountain will do that for you.

Turk sipped his drink. "Hey, can I unzip that pretty dress, baby?"

She sashayed over to him and turned so he could reach the zipper. When he was done, her dress slithered to the floor, leaving her standing before all of us wearing only a lacy black thong and bra and her sky-high heels.

As she walked around, her ass and tits jiggled just enough to get my motor revving, and before I knew it, my dick was like a baseball bat.

"C'mere you," I said, holding my arms out for her.

She sauntered over and straddled me where I sat on the sofa.

Remy and Turk smiled and walked up behind her.

She pressed her lips to mine, something I'd been dreaming about all day. They were soft and sweet, like I knew they'd be, and as we kissed, I inhaled her scent—which was nothing more than clean girl.

Damn, I liked that.

Turk unfastened her bra and had his hands on her fleshy tits in seconds, and Remy climbed up on the sofa next to us and started running a hand over the curves of her ass.

She leaned toward me and whispered in my ear. "I want you to fuck me."

CHAPTER 21

ALESSIA

Forrest laid me down on his king bed, the other guys surrounding us, and pulled my thong to my ankles. He stretched my legs all the way apart and dove between my thighs, licking me from clit to ass and back.

I writhed under him from the pure bliss and the suspense of wanting more. His gaze never left me as he moved up and down my slit, his eyes heavy-lidded with passion.

Turk took one side of the bed, and Remy, the other. They'd both pulled their hard cocks out, so I took Turk's in one hand, and Remy's in my mouth.

Holy crap. I was with three guys.

Poor Dash. I'd have to make it up to him later.

While I stroked Turk and sucked Remy, Forrest grabbed a condom from somewhere and sheathed himself. Kneeling between my legs, he placed a thumb on my hard clit, making small circles, and enjoying the view of my getting worked over by his friends.

He brought my legs together and pushed them straight up in the air with one hand. With the other, he gently opened my pussy, slipping the head of his cock inside. I moaned with my full mouth, and with one thrust of his hips, he drove inside me up to his balls.

Turk and Remy each took hold of one of my legs and held them back as far as they would go while Forrest seized my hips and pounded me with his hard dick.

I was swimming in ecstasy, waves of it holding me afloat as our movements rocked the bed.

"Fuck, baby, your pussy is so beautiful," he said. "Isn't she beautiful, guys?"

They nodded and smiled.

"Fuck yeah. Look how she's sucking me. I'm gonna spurt down her throat any second," Remy groaned.

Just then, Turk pulled himself out of my hand and hovered over my tits to cover them in streams of warm cum. My hands flew to massage it into my heated skin.

At nearly the same time, Remy pulled out of my mouth and unloaded on my tits just like Turk had, growling at the top of his lungs.

My own orgasm hit hard, leaving me thrashing so Turk and Remy had to jump out of the way.

"Fuck me, Forrest," I mumbled. "Fuck me harder."

He ground all the way inside me, and a tickle started in my belly. It quickly spread up my breasts and my neck, and then, everything exploded. I couldn't see, hear, or speak. All I could feel was the pulsing in my pussy, overtaking my entire body.

Forrest drove inside me one more time, his cock hardening even more as he came. We all collapsed on the bed, and next thing I knew, I was surround by slow breathing and light snoring. In the tangle of arms and legs, I couldn't figure whose limbs belonged to whom.

It didn't matter.

I slipped out of bed to grab my vibrating phone and took it to the bathroom to avoid waking the guys.

"Hey, Dash," I whispered, my mouth dry from the night before. "Everyone else is still in bed."

He laughed, and I heard Ozzy whining in the background. "Those guys are bums."

Actually, I think I had worn them out. But I wasn't going to say that and make Dash feel left out.

"Wish you were here," I said.

He sighed. "I wish I were there, too, honey. Hey, when the guys get up, give them the info on where

Mont's new house is. I'll text it to you. He's at work now, but his girlfriend is at home alone."

Mont's girlfriend. The lovely Vanessa. The woman who I'd thought was my friend, who was in my freaking wedding. Well, almost-wedding.

Vanessa was a tall, stunning blonde with a creamy complexion. She'd ignored me in the early part of the show—clearly I wasn't of her caliber. But as things wore on, she'd befriended me like we'd been buddies all our lives.

Only now did I realize that was part of the plan. I was the only idiot not in on it.

And only now did I realize why she'd tried so hard to get me to wear the world's ugliest wedding dress.

She was pissed Monty was marrying me and not her. But in reality, he was hers and always had been.

They could *have* each other. Seriously

I waited for Dash's text to come through while I downed several glasses of water and pulled on jeans, a T-shirt, and my blonde wig.

While contemplating whether I should wake the guys or just hang out till they got their tired asses out of bed, I found myself getting pissed.

Really pissed.

Like *I could kill something* pissed.

Vanessa.

That nasty whore had pretended to be my friend and the whole time was fucking the guy I was supposed to marry.

She was flitting around a comfortable, lavish home, enjoying money that was due *me*.

And she'd gone on national TV and ripped me to shreds like the bitch that she was.

I grabbed my sunglasses to head out.

I had a score to settle and I was the only one who could do it.

But before I left, I took a quick look at the guys, still passed out. God, they were beautiful, naked and sprawled on my giant bed, only partially covered in sheets and blankets. My heart swelled that these amazing men wanted nothing but the best for me. If I could have captured that moment, I would have bottled it and kept it forever.

I ran for the elevator and through the hotel lobby. I told myself I needed to hurry, but if I were really honest with myself, I was running before the guys could realize I was gone and stop me. I knew they were looking out for me because they cared about me—but some things a woman has to do on her own.

I hopped in a taxi and gave the driver Mont's address.

Wouldn't Vanessa be surprised to see me?

I should have known something was off the day of the wedding. Wearing the ugly pink concoction the show had chosen for the bridesmaids, Vanessa was off in a corner sipping champagne and rolling her eyes at the attention I was getting.

The attention I'd never wanted, to begin with.

At my request, the cab dropped me two doors down from the address Dash had provided. I rang the bell and stepped aside so I couldn't be seen through the peephole.

The door flew open and Vanessa looked at me, frowning.

She had no idea who I was.

"Hey, Vanessa."

She tilted her head and realization crossed her face.

"What the hell are you doing here?" she snapped after her initial surprise.

"I wanted to talk to you about something."

She started to close the door. "We have nothing to talk about."

But I wedged my foot inside. "I want what's mine."

"There is no *mine*, you fool. You left the show. You're not supposed to get shit."

"Do you want to be exposed?" I asked. "I'll go to the press and expose the show, the network, and you."

Her eyes widened, and she stepped back. "You can't do that. Billy told us you could never do something like that."

I moved closer to her, pointing. "Well. Now who's the fool?"

"Wh... what do you want?" she asked, breathing hard.

"I want my money."

She shook her head violently. "We don't have any

money to give you. I don't know what you're talking about. You have to take that up with the show."

"Actually, I know you have money, and I know it's right here in this house. So, why don't we go get it, so I can get my share and be on my way?"

Oh, my god. I had no idea I could be so demanding.

I was a badass.

Vanessa just stood there, staring at me.

I shrugged. "Okay. If you can't accommodate me, I'll head out and leave you alone. But not before calling the authorities. And the press."

"Wait—" she sputtered. "Hold on. You can have whatever you want. Come in."

I followed her through her sumptuous house decorated in soft neutrals, not unlike the place I'd shared with Mont.

At least he was consistent in his taste.

But after we'd passed through the dining and the living rooms and climbed the stairs to the bedrooms, my blood really began to boil. I spotted several pieces of furniture we'd gotten together, as well as some that I had brought from my own apartment.

"I gotta get my things out of here at some point," I muttered.

Vanessa turned to me. "Take what you want. I really don't care."

"What I want, Vanessa, is my portion of the half million dollars Mont got from the show. No more, and no less."

We entered a bedroom, and Vanessa dove into a closet where she began working on the combination to a safe built into the wall.

She pulled the door open.

And it was empty.

"See," she said, "there's nothing here."

"I know you have the cash here. I have friends who are very good at getting information. So get out the cash, Vanessa, before I lose my patience."

She stared me down with more hatred than I thought was possible. "You're a fool, Alessia. You should have just gone along with the wedding and gotten your money. All you had to do was ride things out for a year or two, and then, Mont was going to set you free. You would have been a rich woman."

She took a step closer to me, leaving me wishing I had a weapon of some sort to defend myself.

That had been a big oversight.

But Vanessa only wanted to hurt with ugly words. "Did you really think Mont would go for someone like you? Seriously, Alessia?"

My entire body trembled with rage. "You bitch. You were in my wedding. You pretended to be my friend. You're nothing but a cun—"

She got louder. "Oh, come on. Are you the last person in the world to realize reality TV is completely rigged? And those of us who get ahead are the ones who can act?"

Ah. It made sense now. Vanessa and her ilk were on *The Mating Game* hoping to hone their acting chops.

I shook my head at her. "I don't think I've ever heard anything more pathetic in my life. You think you're gonna get into acting via reality TV?" I threw my head back and howled with laughter.

When I caught my breath, I looked at my watch. If Forrest, Remy, and Turk, weren't up yet and wondering where the hell I was, they would be soon.

"Vanessa, my cab is waiting outside. I'll give you thirty seconds to make things happen. Then, I'm leaving. And sharing our story with the world. Hey, maybe you'll become famous after all."

"Bitch," she mumbled and dove deeper into the closet.

I heard the tick-tick of a another combination lock, and then a squeaky door opened. I grabbed an empty gym bag off a shelf and threw it to her.

"Use this. Get going."

Bundles of cash started filling the bag with loud *thumps*, and I began to sweat because my phone was vibrating non-stop in my pocket. Surely, by now, the guys were out of their minds wondering where I was.

So, I called them. "Hey, Turk. I'm at Mont's house,"

I kept one eye on Vanessa.

He hurled a string of expletives so loud, I couldn't even follow him.

"Yeah, Turk, I can't hear you, phone's going dead, talk to ya later."

And I hung up.

"Who can't you hear?" a man entering the room behind me asked.

Oh shit.

That was a voice I knew well.

Mont. No surprise there.

I turned to find he had a gun. Which *was* a surprise. I didn't know he had any thug in him.

Impressive, in a sad sort of way.

"What took you so long, Mont?" Vanessa hissed.

I smiled at my almost-husband. "Mont! How's the nose?"

Vanessa grabbed me by the upper arm and pushed me out of the closet. "Get going."

Being held at gunpoint was new territory for me.

She pulled me down to the kitchen with Mont close on our heels and settled me into a chair.

I struggled but between the two of them, I was easily restrained.

That didn't mean I was going to make their job easy.

"Really, guys? Don't you think you're already in enough trouble? When the show finds out what you and Billy did, you'll have to pay back *all* the money, and your reputations will be *shit*. Isn't it easier to give me my share of the cash and be done with it?"

"Shut up," Vanessa said. She was attempting to tie my hands together with a piece of rope.

But it was obvious she'd never done it before, hold

someone prisoner, and Mont had never pointed a gun at anyone. Sweat was pouring down his temples, and he looked like he might vomit.

But I'd never been in my position either, so to be honest, playing bad guys was new to us all.

Mont grabbed a chair and settled in right in front of me. "Alessia, you are nothing but a pain in the ass," he spat. "You are going to ruin everything. But I won't let you. You had your chance and blew it. You could have just gone through with the wedding and kept your goddamn mouth shut. But you didn't, and now you're pissed."

"You're damn right I'm pissed. You and your cronies," I jerked my head toward Vanessa, "manipulated me like I was a fucking little toy you could use and then throw away. You're a bunch of pathetic slime bags. I hope you rot in hell. All of you."

I inhaled as deeply as I could.

And spat.

Right in his face.

I don't know who was more surprised—Mont or me.

But one thing was certain—he wasn't pleased.

He wound up his arm, and his palm sailed toward my face. I watched it move closer in a strange slow motion while Vanessa's mouth opened and closed, emitting sounds I couldn't make out.

At the exact moment Mont's hand made contact with my face, there was a blur of movement in my peripheral vision. As I was going down, someone belted Mont, sending him flying in the other direction.

And just before I made contact with the floor, two strong arms caught me.

Mont wasn't so lucky.

His gun skittered across the tile as he slammed to the floor with an *oof*.

Vanessa screamed.

I closed my eyes.

The guys had come.

For me.

CHAPTER 22

TURK

W hen I'd woken up in the hotel and Alessia was nowhere to be seen, it hadn't immediately occurred to me that she'd go freaking rogue. I figured she'd just gone down for coffee.

But after I'd returned to my own room in the suite and showered and dressed, it became clear she wasn't returning any time soon.

"Guys, wake up," I said to Remy and Forrest.

They both looked around drowsily.

"Alessia's missing."

Forrest ran his fingers through his hair. "What the fuck? Where the hell did she go this time?"

"I'll call Dash and have him trace her," Remy said.

Not five minutes later we were in our truck, racing toward the same address Dash had given Alessia an hour earlier—Mont's place of residence.

When we got there, the scene in front of us reminded me of playing cops and robbers when I was a kid.

Mont and Vanessa had Alessia tied up at gunpoint. If I hadn't realized it was a real gun, and that Mont probably didn't know shit about shooting, I might have doubled over in laughter. Alessia sat in a kitchen chair with her hands tied behind her back.

"Turk!" she screamed.

It took the guys and me about ten seconds to get the situation under control.

First, Remy got Montgomery by the scruff of his shirt. Then, Forrest grabbed Vanessa by the arm.

I untied the lame knot from Alessia's hands. "God-dammit, what possessed you to come over here alone?"

She rubbed her wrists. "I wanted to take care of Vanessa myself and get my money without help from anyone."

"Fuck you, bitch!" Mont, his face purple with anger, lunged at Alessia.

But he was no match for Remy's grip. And he was a fool for thinking he would be.

Remy twisted his arm up behind his back, just short of causing real damage, leaving him screaming.

"Where's the money, dickhead?" Remy asked.

Before he could answer, Alessia pointed toward the stairs. "Bedroom closet."

I looked at Remy and Forrest. "You guys wait here with these clowns."

I followed Alessia up the stairs two at a time, and she dove into a closet and retrieved a gym bag half-filled with what looked like about two dozen bundles of hundred-dollar bills.

"Wow," I said.

Her expression was solemn. "Can you believe it?"

When we returned to the kitchen, Montgomery was on the floor, screaming, his nose gushing blood, again, just like it had been at the gas station.

I didn't even want to think of the pain he must be in.

Remy stood over him, shaking his head. "It's beginning to look like our friend Mont really likes getting smacked in the schnoz."

A muffled *fuck you* came from the floor.

Not to be left out, Vanessa started at Alessia. "You're such an idiot, you know that—"

But she didn't get to finish.

Alessia planted a full palm on Vanessa's face so hard that she went flying and joined Montgomery on the floor.

She bent over the two of them. "You both need to remember that if you give me any trouble, I will go right to the press and let them know how Billy and you set things up. You'll lose everything."

Vanessa looked up from the floor. "Get out!" she screamed.

"Gladly," Alessia said.

Remy scooped up Montgomery's gun. "This is probably not safe with you. We'll take it off your hands."

When we were back in the car, I asked the question that had been hounding me. "Alessia, if Mont liked Vanessa, why didn't he just choose her?"

She took a deep breath. "Because apparently the audience resonated with me, the girl next door. I guess they were tired of glamazons always getting the guy. So they pushed me front and center and scammed everyone for ratings."

Montgomery was a bigger idiot than I thought.

Everyone knew the girl next door was the sexy one.

The next day, we all moved to a house on the beach, and Dash joined us with Ozzy. Alessia was being very generous with her new nest egg and wanted to show her appreciation to us guys. So, she rented this freaking amazing place with glass windows all across the front, where we could just sit and watch the waves crash for hours on end.

Of course, with the summit coming, we only had a few days to enjoy it.

But still.

"What do you think, guys?" Alessia sashayed out of one of the bedrooms to show off a tiny pink bikini.

Seriously. It was *small*.

"Holy crap," someone murmured.

She did a little spin, and damn if the tiny scraps of fabric barely contained the cheeks of her ass or her lovely bouncing tits.

"Anyone for a swim?" she asked.

Yeah, I wanted to swim. But I had to wait for my goddamn erection to subside. And while it did, I watched our girl grab her towel and skip out the door across the soft sand, where she buried her toes in the warm Pacific Ocean.

CHAPTER 23 AND OTHER STUFF

ALESSIA

Finally.

Finally, I had the money I'd earned from that stupid show, which Billy and Mont had tried to cheat me out of. They might have felt I hadn't earned it because I didn't go through with the actual wedding.

But the way I saw it, I'd *more* than earned it.

So, screw them.

At last, I'd be able to get back to my old life—the boring-ass one where I went to work at a dull job every day—but where I was surrounded by friends who cared about me and wouldn't think of fucking me over the way those guys had.

Eventually, even the press would leave me alone. A new season of *Mates* was starting soon, and they'd be on to stalking some other unsuspecting contestant.

I'd be free to enroll in the classes I'd dreamed about for so long but could never quite pull off. It was always something that got in the way, like money or schedules. But mostly money.

I was thinking of becoming a vet tech. I really did love animals.

However, my victory didn't mean the pain and humiliation of being duped by a fiancé had vanished. But every day, it lessened a little more.

Only one problem remained.

The guys.

After a bumpy start, they'd been good to me. Really good.

And the sex—well, that was some off the charts shit, the likes of which I doubted I would ever experience again. But it was more than that.

I was attached now. They'd unwittingly worked their way into my heart with their kind goodness and commitment to their work and each other. Dangerous as it was, they were brave and did what they believed in.

First, there was Dash, my brainy but hot computer geek.

Then, Forrest, who lost his dad in 9/11 and dedicated himself to keeping other people safe.

Turk was my foster care refugee who wanted nothing more than to finish his education—like me.

And Remy. Beautiful Remy. He'd left behind the security of a wealthy family to follow his dreams—at the steep price of being cast out forever.

If I'd learned anything in recent days, it was that we all had our own stories. The universe gives us all a shit sandwich at some point or other, which we can't get out of dealing with, no matter how hard we try.

Life happens to everyone, and that includes both the good and the bad. No one's exempt. Hopefully, on any given day, there's more good than bad. But there's no guarantee.

That was for sure.

I turned toward the gorgeous beach house I'd gotten us for a few days of fun, while I stood with the warm ocean lapping at my ankles and Ozzy puzzling over the sand. The guys were heading across the sand toward me, each with their long board shorts and towels draped across their necks. If I could have captured that moment and frozen it, the four of them together, all eyes on me, I would have been the happiest girl in the world for all eternity.

But we can't freeze moments, and every day can't be perfect. It just doesn't happen.

And I couldn't be with four guys.

Sure, it had been hotter than hell, all the sexy times we'd had, but in what world does a girl get her own harem?

Not any that I knew of.

Which meant that, in the end, I'd have to pick one.

One. Only one.

How in the hell was I supposed to do that?

I loved them all.

Shit. Did I just say *love*?

No, I'd pack my things and leave as soon as we were back on the mountain. I know they wanted me to stick around for the summit, but it just made no sense.

I was a big believer in 'ripping off the band-aid.' It hurt like hell initially, but it was over fast. That was my plan.

Pack my shit, say goodbye, and get the hell out.

Forrest reached me first, picking me up and twirling me in the waves. I screamed, barely louder than the pounding surf.

"Kiss me," I demanded in his ear.

His lips crashed into mine, and I held on to him for dear life, dizzy from his spinning me on uneven sand.

The other guys had found a Frisbee and were throwing it back and forth, laughing and stumbling on the beach, with Ozzy trying desperately to join in. I grabbed Forrest's hand and pulled us both into the water until we had to dive under the waves. Once on the other side of the breakers, we treaded water.

"Oh, my god, it's been so long since I've been in the ocean. It feels good." I splashed water in Forrest's face.

He play-frowned and swam toward me until I felt his erection bounce against my leg. He reached under the water, parted my thighs, and wrapped my legs around his waist, keeping us afloat with his treading.

Holding him lightly with my legs, I closed my eyes and leaned back in the water to float.

"Damn, baby. You're so beautiful."

"You aren't so bad yourself, mister." I smiled and raised one eyelid just enough to look at the cloudless blue sky. It was a day I'd never forget.

I unwrapped my legs from his waist and led him to shallower water where we could stand. I pulled his hard cock out of his swim trunks after looking around to make sure no one was close by.

He groaned and smiled. "Christ, that feels nice. Sun, water, a beautiful girl. I think I've died and gone to heaven."

He grabbed one of my legs and lifted it up alongside his hip. With his other hand, he teased aside my bikini bottom enough to expose me and began making small circles on my clit.

The surf rocked us back and forth.

"Fuck, baby, I'm gonna come," he groaned as I sped up my strokes.

I pulled him toward me, and we pressed our mouths together. His warm cum exploded through my fingers and into the water around us just as he plunged a finger inside me, making that 'come here' motion. In seconds, I joined him with my own orgasm, gripping him tightly to disguise my shuddering.

Holy crap. There had been a lot of 'firsts' in the last few days of my life.

As we came down, we laughed as we tried to remain upright in the water with the shifting sand under our feet. We held hands and burst through the breakers to get to shore where we found the other guys sprawled on beach towels.

"Damn. I could get used to this," Remy said, looking up and down the beach, the wind ruffling his dirty blond hair.

"Why don't you?" I asked.

He shook his head. "Nah. The mountains are the place for me. Gorgeous as this is, for the kind of work we do, we need a lot of privacy. It's safer in the mountains."

Dash lay back on his towel, hands behind his head, looking very cool in his aviators. "This is great, guys. So glad I joined for the easy part of the trip." He laughed.

"Hey," Remy said, "I almost forgot. I got us a rez at LA's hottest restaurant tonight."

I clapped with glee. "No way! How'd you do that?"

He smiled at me. "Let's just say, Alessia, we know a lot of people."

Forrest slapped him on the back. "You don't know shit, bro. I'm the one with the connections."

"Blah, blah, blah," Remy said, rolling his eyes.

God, I would miss their banter.

And their admiring glances.

And their touch.

"Hey, I think I'm going up to the house to shower and run out for something pretty to wear tonight," I said, throwing my wet towel at Remy.

"Don't be late," he called after me.

~

After employing every primping trick I'd learned on *Mates*, I walked into the living room in my new dress, a silky green wrap number with a plunging neckline that tied at the hip. I couldn't have imagined anything more perfect if I'd tried. It was *exactly* what I'd hoped for.

Apparently, the guys liked it too. There were a couple low whistles and several words of approval.

I took a glass of champagne from Dash. "You guys know how to make a girl feel great. Thank you."

I took a little bow.

A pang of sadness washed over me as I thought about the next chapter in my life and how it probably wouldn't include them.

But maybe it could—on some level.

Dash set his drink down on the table next to the easy chair where he'd sat. "You know, sweetie, there was something we wanted to talk to you about."

"Really?" I looked from one to the other but couldn't get a read on their expressions. "Am I in trouble or something?" I laughed.

Forrest shook his head, *no*. "On the contrary, we have a proposition for you."

My expression must have said *huh?* because he started laughing.

"I'm just gonna cut to the chase," he said. "We're into you. I mean, we like you. A lot. And don't want you to leave. At least, not permanently."

My mouth was suddenly very dry, and a sip of champagne did nothing to help. "Um… well… um…"

That was all I could manage.

Sure, I'd hoped the guys liked me as much as I did them. But asking me to stick around?

I cleared my throat. "You mean, like, I'd be with all of you? I wouldn't have to choose?"

I hoped this was not a joke, because a lump was building in my throat.

"No, babe. You'd be with us all," Turk said.

"And that's okay with you guys?" I asked, hoping.

Four boyfriends.

Four *hot* boyfriends.

Turk nodded. "It is. We discussed it. There'd always be someone looking out for you, say if a couple of us had to go off on a mission. Think of it as insurance."

Remy leaned forward, elbows on knees. "We want you to follow your dreams too. You know, go back to school, and all that. But the mountain would always be your home."

Okay, now I was blubbering like an idiot.

"I… I don't know what to—"

Ugh. Why did I have to be such a crybaby?

Remy crossed the room and took my hand. "Don't feel pressured to make a decision. There's no rush."

My sobs subsided enough for me to take a deep breath.

"You jerks just made me ruin my makeup."

They laughed.

"I accept."

I looked around at each of them, the handsome devils that they were. "I want to be with you because I love you," I said.

Shit, the waterworks started again.

But that didn't stop the guys from jumping up and running over to me while high-fiving each other.

"Fucking A, Alessia. That's incredible."

Someone untied the bow on my dress, and the green silk slithered to the floor.

Our fancy dinner could wait for another night.

EPILOGUE

Remy

Alessia had been good for all us guys in a lot of different ways.

The most important, for me, was that she somehow managed to be a bridge between my parents and me. It wasn't easy at first, and there were times I felt pushed into having a relationship with people I'd long since written off, but she worked her magic and got us all talking, slowly but surely.

I'm not saying we'd be the closest family moving forward, but it was a start. It would take years, if not the rest of our lives, to untangle the hurt that sent us all in our own directions. It was work she convinced me was worth doing.

Even my brother Cap was speaking with them again. Never thought I'd see that day.

Speaking of which, Alessia got us to agree to let her friend Lady visit around the time of the summit. They were both banking on her meeting a guy or two. Or three. Or four.

As for The Mating Game, *word somehow got out that the show was rigged, and it was pulled from the air mid-season. I heard Billy was fired and disappeared from the LA scene in shame and that Vanessa had come to her senses and dumped Mont's ass. She'd even gone as far as writing Alessia a note of apology.*

She was still trying to get on TV.

I never knew exactly how word about the show got out, but when you treat people the way they did, your secrets are not safe.

Not long after the summit, we drove Alessia to town to see her off to the vet tech program she'd chosen two states away. She had her fingers crossed that after she was certified she'd be able to get a gig at the vet's office in town.

We said our goodbyes to our girl.

"Welp," Dash said, "your laptop should be up to snuff for all your schoolwork."

"Thank you, Dash. I really appreciate it," Alessia said with tears in her eyes.

She looked up at me and ran her fingers through my hair. "Bye, Remy. Look out for your little bro, Cap, okay? Oh, and Ozzy too."

I just nodded. I couldn't speak.

Turning to Turk, she pulled off his Ray Bans to get one last look at his famously blue eyes. "See ya soon?"

Last but not least was Forrest, the hardest of us all to win over. But she'd succeeded, just like she did everyone she met with her kindness, humility, and grace. Not to mention burning hot good looks.

She ran her fingers over his neck tattoo and he smiled, his dimples jumping into action. "Bye for now," she said, kissing him lightly.

She boarded the bus to the airport after we threw her two large suitcases in the luggage compartment.

But just before she ran up the steps, she turned to us. "See you guys in six weeks. It's only six weeks. It will go fast."

And she was gone.

I supposed six weeks would go fast, busy as we were. We each had a mission or two that would take us to lands far away. But our hearts would never be far from Alessia, or from Savage Mountain.

We had a funky little family, the five of us. Who knew what the future would hold?

But family was the operative word.

And we had Alessia and she had us. That was all that really mattered.

$\approx$

Get a free short story!
Join my Insider Group

ALSO BY MIKA LANE

The Savage Mountain Men Reverse Harem Series
#1 The Captive
#2 The Runaway
#3 The Pursued
#4 The Prize

Contemporary Reverse Harem
#1 The Inheritance
#2 The Renovation
#3 The Promotion
#4 The Gallery
#5 The Collection
Boxset books 1-5

A Player Romance series 1-3
#1 Mister Hollywood
#2 Mister Fake Date
#3 Mister Wrong

Billionaire Duet 1-2
#1 The Billionaire's Secret
#2 The Billionaire's Betrayal

Stay in the know
Join my Insider Group
Exclusive access to private release specials, giveaways, the opportunity to receive advance reader copies (ARCs), and other random musings.

Let's keep in touch
Mika Lane Newsletter
Email me
Visit me! www.mikalane.com
Friend me! Facebook
Pin me! Pinterest
Follow me! Twitter
Laugh with me! Instagram

ABOUT THE AUTHOR

Dear Reader:

Please join my Insider Group and be the first to hear about giveaways, sales, pre-orders, ARCs, and other cool stuff: http://mikalane.com/join-mailing-list.

Writing has been a passion of mine since, well, forever (my first book was "The Day I Ate the Milky-way," a true fourth-grade masterpiece). These days, steamy romance, both dark and funny, gives purpose to my days and nights as I create worlds and characters who defy the imagination. I live in magical Northern California with my own handsome alpha dude, sometimes known as Mr. Mika Lane, and an evil cat named Bill. These two males also defy my imagination from time to time.

A lover of shiny things, I've been known to try to new recipes on unsuspecting friends, find hiding places so I can read undisturbed, and spend my last dollar on a plane ticket somewhere.

I have several titles for you to choose from including perennially favorite Billionaire stories, and the newer trend in romance, Reverse Harem. And have you see my Player Series about male escorts who make the ladies of Hollywood curl their toes and forget their names? Hottttt.... And my brand new anti-hero/mafia books start coming out next month.

Exciting news: in 2020, I will be publishing with Vi Keeland's and Penelope Ward's Cocky Hero Club as one of their contributing authors. Stay tuned for more on this or follow my Facebook page: https://www.facebook.com/mikalaneauthor.

I'll always promise you a hot, sexy romp with kick-ass but imperfect heroines, and some version of a modern-day happily ever after.

I LOVE to hear from readers when I'm not dreaming up naughty tales to share. Join my Insider Group so we can get to know each other better http://mikalane.com/join-mailing-list, or contact me here: https://mikalane.com/contact.

One last note: Instagram is my guilty pleasure. Please follow me there, and I'll be sure to follow you right back.

xoxo

Love,

Mika